HELLO, MRS. PIGGLE-WIGGLE

BETTY MacDONALD

Pictures by HILARY KNIGHT

HarperTrophy

A Division of HarperCollinsPublishers

Library of Congress Catalog Card Number: 85-43012
ISBN 0-397-31715-8
ISBN 0-06-440149-9 (pbk.)
❖
First Harper Trophy edition, 1985.

CONTENTS

I. THE SHOW-OFF CURE

IT was a beautiful morning. A bluebird sat on a small branch in the flowering cherry tree and swayed gently back and forth. A crocus pushed his golden head through the tender green grass and blinked in the sudden sunlight. Mrs. Carmody hummed as she laid slices of bacon in the black iron skillet. "Spring is my favorite time of year," she said to Mandy the dog who was lying in the kitchen doorway scratching a flea and waiting to trip somebody.

Mrs. Carmody plugged in the toaster, got out the raspberry jam then went to the front hall and called up stairs to her husband, "Jordan, breakfast!" and to her little boy, "Phillip, are you up?"

Phillip who was ten years old and still under the covers, called out sleepily, "Practically all dressed, Mom. Be right down."

Constance, his sister who was eleven and three quarters, yelled from the bathroom where she was testing how lipstick would look when she was thirteen, "Phillip isn't even up, Mom. He won't be down for about ten hours."

Phillip shouted, "Old spy. Tattletale."

Constance said, "Be quiet, little boy. You bore me."

Mrs. Carmody called again louder, "Phillip get out

of bed this instant. Connie, wipe off that lipstick.
Hurry, Jordan, dear, while the toast is hot."

She went back to the kitchen and gave the percolator
a little shake to hurry it up. Then she walked over and
stood by the open back door breathing deeply of the
fragrant early morning air. Her pleasant reverie was
suddenly broken by Mr. Carmody who came grumpily
into the kitchen, tripped over Mandy and stepped heavily into her water bowl which was on the floor beside
the stove.

Mrs. Carmody grabbed the sink sponge and began
wiping up the water.

Mr. Carmody growled, "Well, that's certainly a nice
morning greeting."

Mrs. Carmody said, "Oh, Jordan, dear, I'm so sorry.
Did you get wet?"

"It doesn't matter," said Mr. Carmody mournfully.
"Nothing matters any more."

"What do you mean 'nothing matters any more'?"
asked Mrs. Carmody as she squeezed out the sponge.

"Just that," said Mr. Carmody sadly pouring almost
the whole pitcher of cream on his shredded wheat biscuit.

"Are you sick?" asked Mrs. Carmody peering anxiously at him.

"No, I am not sick," he said. "Or at least I'm not
physically sick. Just sick at heart."

Mrs. Carmody buttered the toast, put the plates in to
warm, stirred the eggs, lifted the bacon on to a paper
towel to drain, checked the color of the coffee, refilled
Mandy's water bowl, then said, "What in the world

are you talking about, Jordan? You don't make sense."

"He makes sense to me," said Connie flouncing into the kitchen. "Because I feel the same way. I'm so ashamed I could die."

"What in the world are you talking about?" said Mrs. Carmody. "Are you ready for your eggs, Jordan?"

"I suppose so," said Mr. Carmody dolefully.

Quickly Mrs. Carmody took the plates out of the oven, divided the eggs into four equal portions, added a dash of paprika, laid on four strips of bacon and two pieces of toast, carried two of the plates to the table and snapped them down in front of her husband and daughter. "Now," she said folding her arms, "tell me what this is all about."

Connie picked up a piece of bacon and began nibbling at it. "Well," she said, "if you really want to know."

"I do," said her mother.

"Well," Connie said, "the point is that Phillip is ruining all our lives and you won't face it."

"Ruining our lives! Phillip?" said Mrs. Carmody. "Don't be ridiculous."

"I'm not being ridiculous," said Connie. "Phillip is such a disgusting little show-off I'm ashamed to bring my friends home any more. What about last night? He disgraced poor Daddy."

Mrs. Carmody gazed at her daughter intently for a minute then said, "Connie, you've got on lipstick again. Go upstairs and wash it off."

"Oh, honestly," Connie sighed heavily. "Every single girl in the whole United States of America wears lipstick but me. I'm just a freak. A poor freak with a disgusting little brother."

"Yes, yes, I know," said her mother. "Go up and wash the lipstick off."

When she was sure she could hear Connie's furious footsteps on the stairs she turned to her husband and said, "Now, Jordan, dear, what is all this?"

Mr. Carmody said, "Meg, Phillip is an obnoxious little show-off. Last night was the worst I've ever seen him, and Bob Waltham is my most important client and frankly I wouldn't blame him if he never came into this house again."

"Oh, Jordan," said Mrs. Carmody laughing. "Phillip was just trying to be entertaining."

"Do you call putting a whole baked potato in his mouth entertaining? Do you call drinking an entire glass of water without stopping, then choking and turning purple and spitting water all over the table entertaining? Do you call looking cross-eyed, touching his chin with his tongue, wiggling his ears, standing on his head, reciting the alphabet backwards and forwards and sideways and upside down, entertaining? Well, I don't. AND NEITHER DID BOB WALTHAM!"

"Now, Jordan," said Mrs. Carmody. "You know that Bob Waltham is a stuffy old bore. You've said so yourself, and after all Phillip is only ten. He's just a little boy. You shouldn't be so hard on him."

"You mean, *he* shouldn't be so hard on *me*," said Mr. Carmody angrily ripping a piece of bread in half.

"Meg, something has to be done about that boy. Now! Today!"

Just then Phillip came rattling down the stairs and skidded into the breakfast room. "Hi, Dad. Hi, Mom," he said cheerfully.

"Morning," said Mr. Carmody grumpily.

"Good morning, Phillip, dear," said Mrs. Carmody.

Phillip sat down, grabbed the sugar bowl and began dumping sugar on his shredded wheat biscuit.

"Not so much sugar, honey," said his mother.

Phillip added two more heaping teaspoons of sugar then dumped the rest of the pitcher of cream on his cereal.

Looking brightly, eagerly at his father he said, "Hey,

Dad, want to watch me put this whole shredded wheat biscuit in my mouth all at once?"

"I DO NOT," said his father.

"Not even if I whistle Dixie with it *in* my mouth?"

"NO!" roared his father.

"Eat your breakfast, dear," said his mother putting a fresh pitcher of cream on the table.

"What if I——" Phillip began.

"STOP TALKING!" bellowed his father.

Connie who had come downstairs and was standing unnoticed in the doorway said, "What a repulsive little show-off! My gosh, Mother, can't you see how disgusting he is?"

"My gosh, Mother, can't you see how disgusting he is?" mimicked Phillip in a high squeaky voice. "Shoot him, Mother! Kill him! Cut him up with the butcher knife. Mommy, he embarrasses me in front of my stupid, ugly, giggling friends."

"Now children," said Mrs. Carmody gently.

Mr. Carmody glared around the table and said fiercely, "I want *absolute quiet!*"

"My gosh, Dad, what's the matter?" asked Phillip. "Are you sick or something?"

"Yes, I'm sick or something," said Mr. Carmody savagely jabbing a spoon into the raspberry jam.

"I'll get you an aspirin," said Phillip sliding out of his chair. "I'll get two aspirins and I'll carry them all the way downstairs on my nose. Watch me."

"SIT STILL!" shouted Mr. Carmody. "Sit still and eat your breakfast and DON'T TALK."

"Well, okay," said Phillip. "But you don't have to be so crabby."

"BE QUIET!" yelled his father.

Phillip gave him a reproachful look, sat down again and began to eat his shredded wheat biscuit.

Mrs. Carmody brought her plate and Phillip's from the kitchen and sat down. She looked out the window at the pale pink cherry blossoms and the clear sky and the fat bluebird swaying on the branch but she no longer felt happy. She took a sip of coffee which was lukewarm and looked around the breakfast table.

Phillip was eating busily but the minute she looked at him he grinned broadly and whispered, "Hey, Mom, want to watch me balance my cocoa cup on my forehead?"

She smiled, shook her head and motioned for him to be quiet.

"Even if it's clear full of boiling hot cocoa?" She shook her head.

"Even if it has the spoon in it?" She shook her head.

"What a bunch of crabpatches," Phillip said.

"QUIET!" bellowed his father.

Phillip reached for the jam dish and began sulkily emptying it on to his plate.

When breakfast was at last over and everyone had left for work or school Mrs. Carmody heated up the coffee, poured herself a cup and sat down at the table to look at the morning paper. Just as she opened the paper the corner of her eye caught a glimpse of something white on the floor under Phillip's chair. She reached over and picked up a small folded piece of paper. She opened it up, smoothed it out and read:

Dear Mrs. Carmody:
  I am having a little difficulty with Phillip. Will

you please call me at your earliest convenience.
Sincerely,
Edith Perriwinkle.

Mrs. Carmody looked at her watch—it was four minutes to nine—perhaps she could get Miss Perriwinkle before the bell rang. She hurried into the hall and dialed the number of the school.

When Miss Perriwinkle heard Mrs. Carmody's anxious worried voice she said, "I didn't intend to worry you Mrs. Carmody—it isn't anything serious—it is just that Phillip has become quite a . . . quite a . . ."

"Show-off," said Mrs. Carmody.

"Well, yes," said Miss Perriwinkle. "I guess that is the right word. I also must admit that he is very entertaining and his little schoolmates think he is very funny and laugh at everything he does. Unfortunately he no longer confines his antics to recess and the schoolyard so I have to take steps. Which is why I wrote the note."

"Well," said Mrs. Carmody, "I should have seen it coming, because we are having our problems with him at home, too. Have you any suggestions?"

"Yes, I have," said Miss Perriwinkle. "I think you should call Mrs. Piggle-Wiggle. You've heard of her haven't you?"

"I've heard the name," said Mrs. Carmody. "Is she some sort of doctor?"

"Oh, my no," said Miss Perriwinkle. "She is just a very nice little woman who loves and understands children and has a very magic way of curing their bad habits. Her telephone is Vinemaple 1-2345."

"Just a minute while I get a pencil," said Phillip's mother.

Of course she couldn't find a pencil but she did finally find a broken green crayon with which she wrote down Mrs. Piggle-Wiggle's telephone number on the back of the gas bill.

Mrs. Carmody's hand was shaking as she dialed the number but Mrs. Piggle-Wiggle had such a warm friendly voice that Mrs. Carmody got right over her nervousness and told her all about Phillip.

Mrs. Piggle-Wiggle laughed and said, "Isn't it a shame that children can't be all evened up? I mean some are show-offs and some are shy and some are quiet and some are noisy and some laugh too much and some cry too much. Oh, I could go on and on but loud or quiet, shy or show-offy, timid or boisterous, children are wonderful and I love them all."

"So do I," said Phillip's mother. "And actually, Mrs. Piggle-Wiggle, Phillip's showing off doesn't bother me. But his daddy says he is obnoxious and his sister Connie says he is disgusting and this morning his teacher Miss Perriwinkle told me that he is getting out of hand."

"Well," said Mrs. Piggle-Wiggle, "if it were only his older sister who complained about Phillip I would be inclined to let time work things out, but as long as Phillip is annoying his daddy and Miss Perriwinkle who is one of the best fifth-grade teachers in this county, then we had better take steps."

"Take steps?" quavered Phillip's mother. "What do you mean by steps?"

"Oh, it's very simple," said Mrs. Piggle-Wiggle.

"Have Phillip come down after school and I'll give him a bottle of Show-off Powder. For the next few days sprinkle a little on him before meals, especially when you are having company, and just before he leaves for school in the morning. I'm sure you won't have any more trouble."

"But what is this show-off powder? Will it hurt Phillip?" asked Mrs. Carmody fearfully.

"Show-off Powder is guaranteed to be harmless," said Mrs. Piggle-Wiggle. "But it will stop showing off. You see it makes the show-off invisible."

"Invisible!" wailed Phillip's mother. "You mean I won't be able to see my own little boy?"

"Not when he's showing off," said Mrs. Piggle-Wiggle matter-of-factly. "Nobody will be able to see him. But when he stops showing off and is normal he'll come back into focus."

"Are you sure?" asked Phillip's mother.

"Oh, my yes," said Mrs. Piggle-Wiggle. "Now don't worry about it, just send Phillip up after school. I know that everything is going to be fine. Good-bye and *don't worry.*"

But Mrs. Carmody did worry. She worried as she washed the breakfast dishes and tidied up the house. She worried as she made out the grocery list and sorted the laundry. But she worried the most when she was straightening up Phillip's room.

"What if this powder makes Phillip disappear and then something goes wrong and he won't come back," she sobbed as she took two apple cores, three funny books, a slingshot and an empty box of Smith Brothers' cough drops out from under Phillip's pillow.

Phillip's room was so messy and she was in there such a long time picking up and imagining terrible things that she finally decided not to send for the magic Show-off Powder. That old powder was far too dangerous to use on a sensitive intelligent little boy like Phillip and anyway Phillip's showing off was really very clever and maybe some day he'd be on the stage. Then the front door crashed open, a loud voice yelled "Mom. Hey, Mom, where are you?" and Phillip was home from school.

Mrs. Carmody rushed downstairs and sure enough there was Phillip very much alive and visible, sitting at the kitchen table wolfing down gingerbread and milk. His back was toward his mother but she could see that one sleeve was ripped out of the sweater. "Phillip," his mother said, "what in the world happened to your sweater?"

"Fell off my bike," Phillip said through a mouthful of gingerbread.

"Oh, sweetheart," his mother said running to him, "did you hurt yourself?"

"Oh, not much," Phillip said. "Kind of tore my pants though and ripped one of my new school shoes. See." He held out one leg and showed his mother a pant leg ripped jaggedly to the knee. He held out the other and showed her his brown oxford with a large tear over the instep. He also had a cut over his eye, a skinned place on his nose and blood on his chin.

"Oh, Phillip," his mother said, "you might have been killed! Were you hit by a car?"

"Uh, uh," Phillip said.

"Did some big boy push you?"

"Gosh, no," Phillip said.

"Well, then what did happen?" his mother asked.

"Oh, nothin'," Phillip drained his glass of milk. "Can I have another piece of gingerbread, Mom?"

"Certainly," said his mother, "but first I want to know about the accident with your bicycle."

"Well," Phillip said, "if you wanta really know. I was sitting in the basket of my bike ridin' down Mission Hill backwards singing 'Polly Wolly Doodle' and I saw the bread truck comin' and I guess I didn't turn soon enough and I ran into the Wallaces' iron fence and I caught my shoe on the pedal and my pants on a picket and I hit my eye on the handle bars and I don't know what else happened. But, boy, you should have heard the kids and that ole breadman laugh!"

"No doubt," said his mother drily. "Now you go upstairs and change your trousers and your shoes. Bring me the trousers to mend. Take the torn shoe down to Mr. Rizotta and ask him if he can put a patch on it. And on your way home stop at Mrs. Piggle-Wiggle's, she has something for me. Do you know where Mrs. Piggle-Wiggle lives?"

"Sure I do," Phillip said. "We play down there all the time. What's she got for *you?*"

"Never you mind," said his mother. "Just don't forget to stop by there. Now scoot."

A little after five-thirty, Mrs. Carmody happened to look out the kitchen window and saw Phillip coming up the drive followed by a crowd of children. On his head he was carrying his shoe, balanced on the toe of the shoe was a small jar, sitting on the jar was a little green frog. When Phillip saw his mother's face at

the window he called out, "Hey, Mom, lookit! Watch me I'm going to jump over the wheelbarrow with all this stuff on my head."

"Phillip, don't," his mother called.

But he couldn't hear her and she watched horrified as he made a run for the wheelbarrow, caught his foot in the garden hose and fell backwards into the rhododendron bush. The small jar from Mrs. Piggle-Wiggle flew up in the air, and landed on the concrete with a crash. Mrs. Carmody dashed out, knelt down and began picking little pieces of broken glass out of the spilled white powder. Having extricated himself from the rhododendron bush Phillip said, "Gee, Mom, I'm sorry I busted it. I didn't mean to."

"Don't talk," his mother said briskly. "Go in and get me a clean white envelope out of my desk and the spatula off the stove. Hurry."

While Phillip was gone Mrs. Carmody carefully pushed the white powder into a little mound and held her hand over it to keep the wind from blowing it away. When Phillip brought her the envelope and the spatula she scooped up all the powder into the envelope. All but about a half a teaspoonful—this she carefully lifted into the palm of her hand and blew at Phillip.

"Hey, what do you think you're doin'?" he said, rubbing his eyes and coughing.

"Something very wise, I'm sure," said his mother.

Just then Mr. Carmody's car turned into the driveway. Immediately Phillip jumped up into the wheelbarrow and yelled, "Watch me, Dad. I'm goin' to stand on my head in the wheelbarrow. I'm goin' to stand on my head and say the alphabet backwards."

Mrs. Carmody looked at the wheelbarrow but it was suddenly empty. There was no one there. Not only that but there was no sound either.

Mr. Carmody got out of the car and said, "Where's Phillip? Wasn't he here just a moment ago?"

"Yes he was," said Mrs. Carmody, smiling a secret smile.

"Well, I want him to put the hose and that wheelbarrow in the garage," said Mr. Carmody.

"I'll tell him," said Mrs. Carmody. "He should be back in a minute or so." She and Mr. Carmody went into the house and closed the kitchen door.

Phillip, quite red in the face from standing on his head in the wheelbarrow and hoarse from reciting the alphabet backwards and forwards, called after them, "Hey Mom and Dad. Lookit me." But they didn't even glance at him. They acted as if they didn't even hear him. "Hey you kids, lookit me," he called to the children who had followed him home from Mrs. Piggle-Wiggle's. But nobody answered. They just turned and walked out of the yard. Slowly he righted himself, climbed out of the wheelbarrow and went into the kitchen.

"How come you and Dad didn't watch my trick?" he asked his mother who was busy at the stove.

She said, "We didn't see you doing any tricks. Now go and put away the hose and the wheelbarrow and sweep up that broken glass. Dinner will be ready in about five minutes and it's your favorite."

"You mean frankfurters and baked beans and brown bread?" Phillip asked.

"That's right," said his mother.

"Hot diggety," said Phillip.

Reaching into the broom closet his mother took out the broom and dustpan and handed them to him. "Here," she said, very relieved that he was visible again. "Sweep up that glass first."

Phillip took the broom, held it up over his shoulders and began making loud zooming noises. "Hey, Mom," he yelled, "watch me, I'm a jet plane. Here I go for a take-off."

As he said "Watch me," he began to disappear—with "take-off" he was gone.

Humming contentedly his mother took the lid off the steamer and poked the brown bread.

At dinner he disappeared three times. The first time was when he turned his chair around, crouched down on the seat and said, "Look at me! I'm a big gorilla in a cage. Toss me a banana somebody." He disappeared just after "toss me."

Mr. Carmody almost jumped out of his chair. "Meg, Meg," he yelled at Mrs. Carmody. "The boy's gone. There must be a trap door under that chair."

"Don't get hysterical, Jordan," said Mrs. Carmody. "He'll be back." And he was, in about two minutes.

The next morning after he was dressed Phillip climbed on the bannister and yelled at Connie, "Hey, Connie, lookit! I'm sliding down the bannister frontwards sitting up." Then he disappeared and didn't come back into focus until everybody else had finished breakfast and his poached eggs were quite cold. His mother noticed he had a large purple bump over his left eye. As he slid into his chair Phillip said, "Nobody in this whole darn family cares what happens to me. My whole skull is probly cracked but a lot you care."

"QUIET!" roared Mr. Carmody.

Mrs. Carmody said, "Eat your eggs dear, it's getting late." As she spoke to him she leaned over and sprinkled some of the show-off powder in his hair.

Turning around and giving her a suspicious look Phillip said, "Whatcha doin' to my hair, Mom?"

"Just smoothing it down," said his mother smiling dreamily.

During geography while Miss Perriwinkle was standing with her back to the class drawing a map on the blackboard, Phillip stood up on his seat, wiggled his ears, looked cross-eyed, looked like an ape and scratched himself, all sure-fire tricks for making his classmates giggle. Nobody laughed at all. In fact nobody even looked at him because he wasn't there.

During recess he put a whole package of bubble gum in his mouth and blew a bubble bigger than his head but even though the children were all right around him nobody pointed or laughed or said one thing. Because of course they couldn't see him. Then the bubble burst and got Phillip's hair and face all gummy, then the children laughed because he was back in focus again

but Phillip didn't think it was funny at all especially when the school nurse rubbed his face and neck and head with benzine which burned.

After school he didn't feel very funny, his head hurt and so did his elbow so he rode his bike home sitting on the seat the ordinary way. Bobby Westover and Billy Markle rode beside him and they talked quite solemnly about baseball, except once when Billy rode fast down Mission Hill with no hands yelling "Help, help, I'm out of control. My engine's conked out—my landing gear's stuck. Call the crash crew." Bobby and Phillip laughed like anything until Mrs. Allen backed out of her garage and almost hit Billy who couldn't stop and ran into a tree.

Mrs. Allen turned pure white and shook and was very mad. She said, "Billy Markle, I'm going to call your mother up and tell her what a little show-off you are! You almost got killed and you almost wrecked my car and you have practically given me a nervous breakdown."

Billy who was crying said, "Well lookit me. My shirt's tore and my nose is bleedin' and my bike's wrecked."

Mrs. Allen said, "Go on into the kitchen. I'll fix you up but don't bleed all over my clean linoleum."

Bobby and Phillip called good-bye to Billy but he didn't hear them. As they rode down the hill around he corner toward Phillip's house, Phillip said, "Poor dumb Billy. What a show-off!"

II. THE CRYBABY CURE

MRS. FOXGLOVE was baking brownies. Thick chewey chocolatey nutty brownies. The kind her four children loved. She slid the last pan into the oven, lifted Solomon the black cat down off the kitchen stool where he was drooling up at Alma Gluck the canary, and sat down herself.

It was a very dreary February day. The sky was gray, the snow in the yard was gray and slushy and a cold raw wind was swooshing around the house. Mrs. Foxglove hoped that the children had not left their galoshes on the school bus and had remembered to put on their mittens. She was especially worried about Melody whose eyes and nose always seemed to be so red and chapped.

She sighed and stroked Solomon who had jumped into her lap. Then she pushed him off onto the floor and opened the oven door. The brownies were baking beautifully. She switched the bottom pans to the top shelf and the top pans to the bottom shelf, then closed the door and put the milk on to heat for the children's cocoa.

She was just stirring in the cocoa when from way down the street she heard a noise like a fire siren. Woo-ooooo°ooooo ooooo, weeeeeeeeeeeeeeeeeeee, bawwwwwwwwwwwww went the noise getting louder and closer. Mrs. Foxglove sighed and opened the back door. Cornell, her oldest boy who was eleven came dashing up the back steps, gave his mother a hug and said, "I smell brownies. Zowie!"

Harvard, who was nine, stamped the snow off his galoshes and said, "Another hundred in spelling, Mom. How many brownies can I have?"

Emmy, who was six, said, "I lotht another tooth today but I can chew brownieth. How many can I have?"

Melody who was eight came shuffling up the walk her mouth so wide open her mother could almost see her stomach. "Moooooother," she bawled. "The kids are teasig be. Baaaaaaaaaaaaaaaaaaa.aaw."

Mrs. Foxglove said, "Hurry up, Melody, I want to shut the back door before the house gets cold."

"I cad't hurry," Melody sobbed as she wiped her red nose on her sleeve. "I fell dowd and by dee hurts so I cad hardly walk."

"All right then," said her mother. "I'll shut the door and you can take as long as you like." She closed the door.

Instantly a wail like a dying hyena filled the air and Melody came charging up the back steps and threw herself against the back door yelling, "Let be id. I'b freezig."

Mrs. Foxglove opened the door and Melody who had been leaning heavily against it fell into the kitchen. Emmy and Harvard and Cornell who were sitting on the floor taking off their galoshes laughed uproariously. Melody lay stretched out on the floor like a squashed spider bawling. Mrs. Foxglove pushed her aside a little with her foot and shut the door.

Immediately Melody screamed, "You kicked be. By owd mother kicked be."

Mrs. Foxglove said, "Melody, dear, I only pushed you a little with my foot so I could close the door."

Solomon walked over and licked her ear with his rough little tongue.

"Ouch," she shrieked. "Solobon scratched be. Right here on by ear."

"He did not," Emmy said. "He jutht licked your ear. You old bawl-baby."

"By ear, it's bleedig," Melody snuffled. "I'll probably get rabies."

"Gee, Mom, isn't she awful?" said Cornell. "She's the biggest baby in the whole school. Nobody likes her."

"They do so," said Melody sitting up and wiping her eyes with her mittens."

"Aw they do not," said Harvard. "They call you Old-Wet-Washrag-Foxglove."

"That's what *you* call be," said Melody. "Did you hear that, Mommy? He calls be Old-Wet-Washrag-Foxglove all the tibe." She began to cry again.

Mrs. Foxglove said, "Oh, my goodness I smell the brownies. Out of my way everybody. Pick up your things and take them into the coat closet."

The children gathered up their galoshes and coats and mittens and caps and hurried out of the kitchen. All but Melody who was lying on her back on the floor her mittened hands scrunched into her eyes, crying.

Mrs. Foxglove opened the oven door, pulled out a pan of brownies and poked a broom straw down into it. The broom straw came out clean and so she knew they were done. The cocoa was almost boiling so she took it off the burner and set it aside. She was setting out the cups when she noticed Melody. She said, "Come on, chickabiddy. Stop that snuffling and take off your things. The brownies are all done."

Melody hiccupped several times but didn't move.

Mrs. Foxglove reached down, took hold of her arms and lifted her to her feet.

Melody bellowed, "Ouch, ouch, you're hurtig be."

Her mother gave her a little shake. "I am not hurting you and I'm good and tired of your being such a big crybaby." She took Melody by the shoulders, turned her in the direction of the front hall and gave her a little push.

Melody crumpled into a soggy ball and began to sob hysterically, "You're so bead to be I cad't sta'd it. You shake be and jerk be and push be."

"Oh, go up to your room and stay there until you can be cheerful," said Mrs. Foxglove crossly. "Now scat."

Snuffling and glupping Melody went. Only she didn't scat. She shuffled very very slowly.

Her mother watched until she reached the doorway then sighing with exasperation went back and began pouring the cocoa.

Emmy came skipping into the kitchen. She hugged her mother around the knees and said, "You're the best Mommy in the whole world. Can I have sixth brown-ieth?"

Her mother bent down and kissed her on top of her

head and said, "Let's start with one."

Then Harvard and Cornell came in with Hiboy, the dog, and for a while Mrs. Foxglove was so busy that she didn't have time to think about Melody. Then the telephone rang and it was Mrs. Popsickle and she wanted to know if Emmy and Melody and Cornell and Harvard could all come to her twins', Trent and Tansy, birthday party next Saturday. Mrs. Foxglove said certainly they would love it and Mrs. Popsickle said they were to wear play clothes and come at eleven because Mr. Popsickle was going to take them to Playland and then to a movie.

As soon as Mrs. Foxglove hung up the phone the children all sounding like owls began whoing and whatting and whenning and when Mrs. Foxglove told them that it was a birthday party on Saturday which was only the day after tomorrow, and that they were going to Playland *and* a movie the boys whistled through their teeth and said Zowie and Hot Diggety and Emmy said, "I'm going upstairs right now and get Bruno all dressed."

"Oh, Mom," Cornell said, "don't let her take that dumb old teddy bear. All his stuffing's hanging out."

Emmy said, "I take Bruno every place I go, Mithter Cornell, and he can't help it becauth hith thtuffing is coming out. Tho there."

Harvard said, "Oh, tho there yourthelf!"

Quickly Mrs. Foxglove said, "Boys, I want you to go down and finish up that play table you're making me. But remember, put *all* of Daddy's tools away when you finish."

"I will," Harvard said. "I always do. It's old

Cornell that always leaves stuff out."

"Oh yeah?" Cornell said. "What about the hammer you left over at Fetlock Harroway's?"

"Come boys," said Mrs. Foxglove. "You'd better get started it's almost four-thirty."

When the cellar door had closed behind the boys Mrs. Foxglove turned to Emmy and said, "Emmy, dear, if you'll run upstairs and get Bruno I'll sew his stuffing back in and while I'm doing that perhaps you would like to wash and iron his clothes."

After Emmy had gone upstairs Mrs. Foxglove was scrubbing out the cocoa pan when she heard somebody sniffing behind her. She turned to find Melody, her eyes swollen to tiny slits, her nose as red as a radish, her cheeks blotchy, her lips dry and cracked, standing in the doorway. Melody said, or rather choked out, "I dotice you're washing the cocoa pad and I didn't get ady and I suppose the browdies are all gode, too."

"Your cup of cocoa is right there on the breakfast table," said her mother cheerfully. "And there are lots and lots of brownies in the cookie jar. However, you can't have anything until you wash your face and cheer up."

"I dod't thick I want adythig adyway," Melody said sadly and went back upstairs.

Mrs. Foxglove groaned. What was she going to do with Melody? What was the matter with her? Perhaps she had better call Dr. Pillsbury. She went in to the back hall and dialled Dr. Pillsbury's number. His nurse answered and said he was busy but would call her back in a few minutes. Emmy came in. From one hand she was dragging Bruno by one leg, from the other a laundry bag of his dirty clothes. Mrs. Foxglove sent her upstairs for her workbasket and then the phone rang and it was Dr. Pillsbury who, when he heard about Melody, said that he would stop by on his way home.

Bruno was all mended with new black shiny shoe-button eyes and Mrs. Foxglove was ironing his best blue-and-white-checked rompers and the boys were sanding the play table with the electric sander when Dr. Pillsbury arrived. He said, "What a busy happy family. Do you happen to have a cup of hot coffee, Martha?"

"Made it especially for you," Mrs. Foxglove said handing Emmy the rompers and turning off the iron. "Take Bruno and his clothes upstairs and tell Melody to come down."

As she poured Dr. Pillsbury his coffee and put some brownies on a plate she said, "Tim, I'm awfully worried about Melody. She cries all the time over everything. Do you think it could be rheumatic fever?"

"Does she have a fever?" asked Dr. Pillsbury taking two brownies.

"No, she doesn't," said Mrs. Foxglove. "In fact she seems very well but she is so sad. *Everything* makes her cry. She cries so much and her face is so red and swollen all the time she looks as if she had been stung by a million bees."

Dr. Pillsbury slowly stirred his coffee and said, "If I can find nothing wrong with Melody physically, then I would suggest that you call Mrs. Piggle-Wiggle."

"Will she know what to do?" Mrs. Foxglove asked.

"She certainly will," said Dr. Pillsbury. "She knows more about children than anybody in this town."

"Well, I know she cured Cornell's table manners and she stopped Emmy's tattling but I didn't dream she could do anything about crying."

"I'll bet she can," said Dr. Pillsbury. "My goodness, Martha, these brownies are so good it's criminal. I want you to make me a solemn pledge you won't give Eunice the recipe. I'm much too fat as it is."

Mrs. Foxglove laughed and looked very happy, then Melody came shuffling and snuffling downstairs. By this time her face was sort of purple plum color, her nose was like a ripe strawberry, and her mother couldn't see her eyes at all.

Dr. Pillsbury said, "Come here so I can see how heavy you are."

Slowly, slowly, hiccupping with every step Melody walked over to him. He lifted her up and sat her on his knee. Then he said, "Whew, you're quite a chunk for eight years old! Stick out your tongue."

Dr. Pillsbury looked at her tongue, looked down her throat, looked in her ears, listened to her lungs and heart, poked at her stomach and took her temperature. When he had finished he said, "Sound as a nut except for a very advanced case of acute eight-year-old saditis. Better call Mrs. Piggle-Wiggle before a certain party's tear ducts wear out."

After Dr. Pillsbury had gone Mrs. Foxglove sent Melody and Emmy next door to Mrs. Rocket's house to borrow an onion, while she called Mrs. Piggle-Wiggle.

Mrs. Piggle-Wiggle laughed when she heard about Melody and said, "Oh, I've got the most wonderful cure for crybabyitis. It's a tonic that tastes delicious, sort of like vanilla ice cream with caramel sauce, and it works very quickly. In fact if you would send Harvard and Cornell over for it right now, I think we could have Melody cured before Trent and Tansy Popsickle's birthday party Saturday."

"Oh, do you think so?" asked Mrs. Foxglove almost crying herself, she was so happy.

"Certainly do," said Mrs. Piggle-Wiggle. "Tell the boys I sent in and got those new Super Secret Outer Space Other Hemisphere Ten Way Wrist Communicators they wanted. That will make them hurry."

"Oh, thank you, thank you, dear Mrs. Piggle-Wiggle," said Mrs. Foxglove.

"Tell the boys to hurry," said Mrs. Piggle-Wiggle. "It's getting dark and the streets are slippery."

When Mrs. Foxglove called to Harvard and Cornell and told them she wanted them to run an errand for her they groaned and said, "Way over there, golleee" and "My Gosh, just when we're busy sandin' this ole table" and "Why can't somebody else in this family ever run any errands?" Then she told them about the Super Secret Outer Space Other Hemisphere Ten Way Wrist Communicators and they were upstairs jamming on their galoshes and coats in two seconds.

Then Melody and Emmy came back from Mrs.

Rocket's with the onion and Melody was bawling because she had gotten slush in her galoshes and Mrs. Rocket's dog had jumped on her and it was too cold outside and her eyes hurt.

Mrs. Foxglove helped her off with her coat and took her upstairs and put cold cloths on her eyes. The cloths weren't very cold but Melody screamed in pain each time her mother touched her until Mrs. Foxglove finally said, "I declare you must *like* to look like a stewed tomato."

Emmy laughed but Melody immediately began to cry. Mrs. Foxglove sent her to her room to stay until dinner was ready.

When Mr. Foxglove came home he was very cheerful especially when he found that Mrs. Foxglove had chicken and dumplings for dinner. Then Melody came sobbing down stairs to report that somebody had used her toothbrush, she could tell because it was wet.

Her daddy said, "Are you sure it isn't just wet with tears?"

Melody said, "After all, Daddy, I dod't brush by eyes with by toothbrush."

"Very logical," he said putting his arm around her, "but of late you have been as soggy as a bath sponge and dampness rubs off, see?" He held her off so she could see the big wet spot on his jacket where her head had rested.

"In fact," he said as he rubbed at the spot, "you are one of the juiciest children I've ever cuddled."

Melody began to bawl. Opening her mouth wide and scrubbing at her eyes.

Mr. Foxglove handed her his handkerchief and said, "Come on now, Missy, that was only a joke and you know it. Dry those eyes or the place where they used to be and let's have dinner. Where are the boys?"

"They'll be here in a minute, Juniper, in fact I hear them now," said Mrs. Foxglove.

Cornell and Harvard burst in the back door, their cheeks crimson from the cold, their eyes dancing with excitement. Thrusting their wrists at their mother they said, "Mom, just look what Mrs. Piggle-Wiggle sent away and got for us. Super Secret Outer Space Other Hemisphere Ten Way Wrist Communicators. Aren't they keen? Lookit, see all the signs of the zodiac and the dials."

Mrs. Foxglove looked at the SSOSOHTWWC and said, "Now for heaven's sake be very careful how you use those things. I don't want to be deluged with people from another planet."

"Oh, don't worry, Mom," Harvard said. "We got all the directions right here in this little book."

"Didn't Mrs. Piggle-Wiggle give you something else?" asked Mrs. Foxglove.

"Oh, yeah, she gave us this little bottle," Cornell said as he rummaged through the pockets of his jacket taking out nails, string, four peanuts, two rocks with gold in them, a note to his mother telling her about a PTA meeting which had happened two weeks ago and to which she had gone anyway, several nuts and bolts, two gray licorice drops and finally a small bottle wrapped in brown paper.

After she had sent the boys up to wash Mrs. Fox-

glove carefully unwrapped the bottle. It was labeled
"CRYBABY TONIC—one teaspoonful as needed."
Mrs. Foxglove pulled out the cork and smelled it. It
smelled delicious. She called Melody who was standing in the front hall dabbing at her streaming eyes with
her father's handkerchief, to come out to the kitchen.
She poured the tonic into a rather large teaspoon and
very briskly told Melody who was leaning mournfully
against the stove, to open her mouth.

Melody began to cry. "I don't wad to take ady bad
tastig bedicid," she sobbed. "I'b dot sick."

"This isn't bad tasting, it's delicious," said her
mother taking advantage of her opened mouth to force
the spoon in.

Melody gulped down the medicine and then said,
"Id's good. I like id. Cad I have sob bore?"

"Not now," said her mother. "Perhaps another teaspoon before you go to bed. Now help me carry in the
salad plates."

The first thing Mrs. Foxglove noticed about the ef-
fect of the Crybaby Tonic was that all the redness and
swelling disappeared from Melody's face.

"She's probably already cured," thought her mother
happily.

The chicken and dumplings were delicious. Everybody was having a very good time until Cornell who sat
next to Melody sneaked a chicken bone down to Hiboy
who was *never* supposed to be fed at the table but was
usually lying under it ready in case somebody should
spill. Anyway in reaching for the bone Hiboy put one
paw on Cornell's knee which was covered with jeans,

and the other on Melody's knee which was bare. Hiboy didn't mean any harm but dogs do have toenails and he may have scratched her a little but certainly not enough to warrant the banshee howl she let out. "Owwwwww-wwww, woooooooooooow, weeeeeeeee!" she wailed.

Then the strangest thing happened. Out of her eyes gushed two regular faucets of tears. They filled her dinner plate with water, soaked her table mat, soaked her napkin, made a little lake in her lap, poured down her legs and filled her shoes. In fact in no time at all there was a huge puddle around her chair.

"My gosh, Mom, look at old Melody," said Cornell, his eyes as big as dollars.

"Mom, Dad, quick stop her," said Harvard as Melody's gushing tears ran across the table and into his lap.

"Melody, you big dummy," said Emmy, "you've cried all over Bruno'th clean romperth."

Mrs. Foxglove said, "Juniper, do something quick! The water's clear over here under my chair."

Mr. Foxglove yelled at Melody who was now soaking wet from head to toe, "Stop crying. Close your mouth. Smile!"

Melody did and the tears stopped. Everybody stared at her in wonder. "I've never seen so many tears in my whole life," her father said. "How in the world did you do it?"

"I don't know," Melody said. "I just started to cry and the tears came out."

"I'm going to rent you out to water lawns," her daddy said.

"Salt water kills grass," Cornell said.

Mrs. Foxglove said, "Instead of talking nonsense let's all get busy and wipe up this water."

After everything had been wiped off and dried out as much as possible, Melody went upstairs and changed into her pajamas and bedroom slippers, and her mother gave her another plate of dinner. The rest of the meal was devoted to talking about Melody's amazing new achievement. By the time it was over she began to feel very important. In fact she didn't see any reason why such a remarkable child should help with the dishes.

Harvard said, "Listen, Wet Washrag, it's your turn to do the pots and pans."

Melody said, "Don't you dare call me Wet Washrag, Harvard Foxglove, or I'll tell Daddy that you broke

Mr. Maxwell's greenhouse window."

Cornell said, "If you tell on Harvard, Melody, I won't take you on the roller coaster with me next Saturday when we go to Trent and Tansy's party."

"What party?" asked Melody.

"The party Mrs. Popsickle is giving for Trent and Tansy's birthday and Mr. Popsickle is taking us all to Playland and to a movie show," Emmy said. "And it *is* your turn for the pots and pans, Melody, you know it is, it's right on the chart."

"Oh, all right," Melody said.

Everything was going very well until Harvard and Cornell started duelling with two big spoons and in jumping around Cornell stepped hard on Melody's toe. She opened her mouth like a yawning hippopotamus and began to bawl. Instantly two faucets of tears gushed out of her eyes and soaked her pajamas, bedroom slippers, Emmy's dish towel, and Solomon who was rubbing against her legs.

"Help, help, Daddy, make her stop," yelled the boys.

"Smile," shouted Emmy.

"Ooooooooooooooooooo, wooooooooo!" she wailed and the tears poured out faster and pretty soon the kitchen floor was covered with water.

Then Mr. Foxglove came striding out and pushed Melody over to the sink and held her there so her tears would go down the drain. He told Melody to stay there by the sink until she decided to stop crying. She wailed, "But I'b all wet. I'll catch deumodia and die."

"That is your problem," said her father coldly. "You can either stop crying, smile, stop the tears and change into dry things or you can spend the rest of the night standing there at the sink."

Mr. and Mrs. Foxglove were playing Scrabble, Emmy was asleep and Harvard and Cornell were supposed to be doing their homework, when Melody finally stopped crying and sloshed upstairs to change into dry pajamas and slippers. When she finally came down to say good night, her mother took hold of her chin, looked at her anxiously and said, "Do you feel all right, dear?"

Melody smiled rather sheepishly and said, "I feel kind of cold but not a bit sick."

Her mother kissed her and told her to go in the guest room and get Grandmother Dowson's down quilt.

Mr. Foxglove kissed her and said, "For heaven's sake, don't cry in your sleep. You'll drown."

Melody slept well and the next morning when she awakened she felt very happy especially when she remembered that the next day was the birthday party, and the next day after that was Sunday and Pergola Wingsproggle was going to give her a yellow kitten. Also the sun was shining. Also that tonic her mother gave her before breakfast was so delicious.

Everybody was cheerful at breakfast and Mrs. Foxglove told the children she would drive them to school and would drive Daddy to work as she had to have the car. All the children were smiling when they got out of the car at school and Mrs. Rexall, the principal, said to Old Joe, the janitor, "I'm delighted to see that little Melody Foxglove has at last cheered up."

Melody was very cheerful all morning and she got

one hundred in spelling and an A on her story about "My Kitten." Then came lunchtime. She and Emmy and Kitty Wheeling and Susan Gray and Sally Franklin were all sitting together at a table giggling and whispering and having fun when Benji Franklin who was a great tease, leaned over from the table where he was sitting and grabbed Melody's gingerbread.

Without even thinking about the night before Melody opened her mouth and began to cry. Immediately the tears poured out. They filled up her soup bowl, soaked her peanut butter and jelly sandwich, soaked Emmy's sandwich, filled her lap with water, poured onto the table and made a river that flowed into Kitty Wheeling's gingerbread and then into her lap.

The children all began to yell, "Look at Melody. Look out for the tears. Move over I'm getting wet. Help, a flood. Call the fire department!" and other silly things.

Melody got up and ran sobbing out of the lunchroom down the hall and out into the play court which was empty. There was nobody there because they were all inside eating lunch. Melody stood right in the middle of the court and cried and cried and cried and cried. She cried because she was wet. She cried because Benji took her gingerbread. She cried because she was alone. But mostly she cried because it was her habit to open her mouth and bellow when any tiny thing didn't suit her.

Well, she cried and cried and cried and pretty soon the whole courtyard was flooded and the water was up past her ankles. She didn't care she hated everybody and everything in the whole world. She cried and cried and cried. Pretty soon the water was clear up to her waist and lunchtime was almost over and little Emmy was up in the schoolyard which was much higher than the play court, calling down to her, "Smile, Melody. Smile quick or you'll be drownded."

Melody sobbed, "I cad't sbile. I'b too sad." Gallons and gallons more tears rushed out.

Then Kitty Wheeling called down, "Melody, quick, stop crying it's almost time for the bell."

"I dod't care," cried Melody. "I dod't like school adyway." The tears were almost up to her chest now.

Then Pergola Wingsproggle and Emmy and Kitty and Sally and Susan and Mrs. Rexall began whispering and pretty soon Pergola disappeared. Melody kept crying. The tears were almost up to her chin. And then Pergola called out to her, "Melody, quick, look what I've brought you."

Melody looked and Pergola was holding up a darling little orange kitten.

"A kitten. A little kitten of my very own," Melody said and she stopped crying and smiled. The tears stopped. Slowly she made her way across the play court. Once she tripped and had to swim dog paddle. When she finally got out, Pergola showed her the kitten which she couldn't hold because she was too wet. It was adorable with long soft hair and big round blue eyes. She said, "Oh, Pergola, thank you, thank you. It's adorable."

Mrs. Rexall said, "Here, I'll carry it for you, Melody. Now come with me to the teachers' room. I'll dry

you off and Old Joe can dry your clothes down by the furnace. The rest of you children can skip along to class."

After she had taken off her wet clothes, Mrs. Rexall dried her off with a towel and wrapped her in a blanket. Then she handed her the kitten and told her to lie there on the couch until her clothes were dry.

The kitten curled up inside Melody's arm and the blanket was soft and warm and pretty soon they were both asleep. She woke up when Mrs. Rexall came in with her clothes all wrinkly but dry and then there was Mommy to drive the children home and school was over.

That night when Melody kissed her mommy and

daddy good night she said, "I'm never going to cry again. No matter what happens. Not ever." And she never did. *And* at Trent and Tansy Popsickle's birthday party Melody and Betsy Wilt were in the Ferris wheel and something happened to the motor and the Ferris wheel stopped and wouldn't start and there they were right on the very top. Both the little girls were awfully scared but when Betsy began to cry, Melody said, "Crying never helped anything, Betsy. As long as we're up so high, let's see if we can see our houses. Look, way over there, past the saw mill chimney and right up behind the school, isn't that your house?"

Betsy wiped her eyes on her sleeve and looked where Melody was pointing and sure enough it did look like her house. Then she noticed that she could see Little Willow Lake. Then she saw the building where her father worked. Then they both thought they saw Melody's house.

"And I think I see my kitten, Butterball, asleep on the garage roof," Melody said. Just then the Ferris wheel started.

When they got off Mr. Popsickle was waiting for them. He said, "What, no tears? By George, such bravery deserves an ice-cream soda. What flavor will it be, ladies?"

"I'll take chocolate with chocolate ice cream," Melody said.

"Me too," said Betsy. "I've already had strawberry and vanilla."

While they were eating their sodas Mr. Popsickle said, "I thought girls always cried when they were scared."

"I did cry," Betsy said. "But Melody said that crying never helped anything."

"It doesn't either," Melody said. "I know because I used to cry a lot when I was littler."

III. THE BULLY

NICHOLAS SEMICOLON was ten years old. He was a husky boy, very strong and large for his age. All parents like to have large healthy children and Mr. and Mrs. Semicolon would have been very proud of Nicholas except for one thing. One shameful thing. Nicholas was a bully. He hit children littler than he was. He teased and hit girls. He teased and hit puppy dogs. He scared cats. He even threw stones at birds and once he tipped over the stroller of a one-year-old baby left outside the grocery store.

For a long time Mr. and Mrs. Semicolon didn't know about Nicholas. They knew he was large for his age. They knew his friendships with other children didn't last very long. They knew he had not been asked to several birthday parties. But they thought that Nicholas was big and strong and handsome and needed older more intelligent children to play with. In fact just the night before this story opens after Nicholas had kicked the cat, stepped on Josephine, the dog's tail and gone swaggering up to bed, Mrs. Semicolon said to Mr. Semicolon, "Forthright, have you noticed how fine and big and strong little Nicky has grown?"

Mr. Semicolon who was reading about stocks and bonds in the evening paper said, "Sure outgrows his shoes fast. Two new pairs last month."

"I know," said Mrs. Semicolon dreamily, "his feet are just enormous. They're almost as big as yours."

"Good," said Mr. Semicolon brightening up. "Maybe he can wear out those oxblood brogues I got in Chicago last winter. They never did fit and I paid a lot for them."

"Do boys wear brogues?" asked Mrs. Semicolon.

"What difference does it make?" said Mr. Semicolon. "They're shoes and they're new. After all Abe Lincoln went barefoot."

"But, Forthright, dear," said Mrs. Semicolon anxiously, "Nicky is a patrol boy and he needs new patrol boots."

"Nonsense," said Mr. Semicolon. "Shoes are shoes. They are only meant to keep your feet off the cold ground."

The next morning rather hesitantly Mrs. Semicolon went into Nicholas' room carrying the large sturdy brogues. She said, "Look what Daddy got in Chicago, dear."

Nicholas took one of the shoes, examined it carefully then to his mother's surprise said, "Zowie, what strong shoes! Can I wear 'em to school today?"

"I was thinking more of Sunday school," said his mother, "but I guess one day at school won't matter."

Nicholas who was still in his pajamas slipped a bare foot into one of the shoes. He smiled happily. "Kind of big but boy they're strong and heavy."

Mrs. Semicolon heaved a sigh of relief and went downstairs to make the pancakes.

When Nicholas came clumping in to breakfast Mr. Semicolon said, "New shoes, eh, son?"

"Yeah," said Nicholas. "New and strong. I bet if I kicked with these ole shoes it would just about break somebody's leg."

Mr. Semicolon who was reading the paper and not listening said, "Mmmmmmmmmmmmmmmm."

Mrs. Semicolon who was turning the pancakes said, "How many sausages, Nicky dear?"

"Ten sausages and fourteen pancakes," said Nicholas gulping down his orange juice.

"My what a big strong hungry boy you are," said his mother happily.

Then breakfast was over and Nicholas had gone clumping off to school in his new shoes that really didn't fit and Mr. Semicolon had left for the office in his new shoes that did and Mrs. Semicolon poured herself a hot cup of coffee and sat down at the telephone to call up her friends. She had finished talking to Mary Hex when the telephone rang. It was little Roscoe Eager's mother and she was so mad she was choking. She said, "Carlotta Semicolon, if you don't do something about that big bully I'm going to call the sheriff."

"What big bully?" asked Mrs. Semicolon innocently.

"What big bully!" shrieked Mrs. Eager. "You know perfectly well what big bully."

"I don't either," said Mrs. Semicolon. "I don't know any big bullies."

"Oh, yes you do," said Mrs. Eager, "because the biggest meanest cruelest bully in the whole United States is your own son, Nicholas Semicolon."

"You mean my Nicky?" asked Mrs. Semicolon.

"Yes, your Nicky," said Mrs. Eager. "This morning on his way to school he kicked little Roscoe in the shins with his big new shoes and now Roscoe is home lying on the davenport with bandages clear up to his knees and his legs are still bleeding and for all I know both leg bones are shattered."

"How horrible," wailed Mrs. Semicolon. "How terrible. Shall I call the doctor?"

"I already have," said Mrs. Eager coldly. "He's on his way over. But what I want to know is what you intend to do about Nicholas."

"I'll punish him of course," said Mrs. Semicolon, "but I just can't understand it. It doesn't sound a bit like Nicky."

"But it does," said Mrs. Eager. "It sounds exactly like him. Hitting children littler than he is. Kicking dogs. Jerking toys away from babies. Tipping over little girls' tricycles. Pulling cats' tails. Now I have to go, I hear Roscoe moaning for me."

"Jessie, dear, I'm so sorry," said Mrs. Semicolon. "I'll come right over and bring some coloring books and some sugar cookies I baked yesterday."

At first after she hung up the phone Mrs. Semicolon cried a little, then she remembered the new brogues, blew her nose, wiped her eyes and called Mr. Semicolon.

When he answered she said angrily, "Well I hope you're happy!"

"About what?" he asked.

Mrs. Semicolon began to cry. "It's those darned old brogues that didn't fit Nicky anyway," she sobbed.

"What in the world is the matter?" said Mr. Semicolon.

So, Mrs. Semicolon told him about Mrs. Eager's telephone call.

Mrs. Semicolon said, "It never would have happened if it hadn't been for those brogues. I'm going to give them to the Goodwill."

Mr. Semicolon said, "Listen to me, Carlotta dear, it is not the shoes that are at fault, it is Nicky. After all the shoes didn't grab his feet and force them to kick a little boy in the shins, did they?"

"No, I guess not," sniffed Mrs. Semicolon.

"Well, then," said Mr. Semicolon, "the important thing is not the kind of shoes he kicked with, it is the fact that he kicked and a boy smaller than he. Isn't that right, dear?"

"Yes," said Mrs. Semicolon.

"Well, then," said Mr. Semicolon, "when young Nicholas comes home from school you send him up to his room to think things over and I will deal with him when I come home."

Then Mrs. Semicolon remembered about kicking the dogs, jerking toys away from babies, tipping over little girls' tricycles, pulling cats' tails. So she said, "But kicking with the brogues isn't the only thing, Forthright. Mrs. Eager also told me . . ." and she told him all the rest of Nicky's bad actions.

When she had finished Mr. Semicolon said, "I won't *have* a bully for a son. I think I'll go over to school right now and deal with that young man."

"What will you do?" asked Mrs. Semicolon faintly.

There was a pause, quite a long pause on the other end of the wire, then Nicky's father said, "Why don't you call Mrs. Piggle-Wiggle?"

"Oh, Forthright, how clever of you," said Nicky's mother. "I'll call her right away. She'll know just what to do. She always does."

A few minutes later Mrs. Piggle-Wiggle, who was out in her back yard gathering hazel nuts for her two gray squirrels, Taylor and Philbert, heard the phone ring. When she picked it up and said hello, the voice on the other end was so sad and ashamed when it said,

"Hello, Mrs. Piggle-Wiggle," that she knew at once who it was.

Then Mrs. Semicolon started to tell her about Nicky's kicking and hitting and jerking and pushing and tripping little children, but Mrs. Piggle-Wiggle said in her very gentle voice, "I know, Mrs. Semicolon. You don't have to tell me. I know all about it."

"Do you mean the other mothers have called you up?" said Mrs. Semicolon.

"No, no," said Mrs. Piggle-Wiggle, "but Nicky has been coming over here to play for a long time. I've watched him grow from a rather sickly weak child into a fine, strong, healthy boy. You should be *proud* of him, Mrs. Semicolon."

"I was," said Mrs. Semicolon, "until this morning. Now, after what I have heard I wish he was sickly and weak still."

"Not really," said Mrs. Piggle-Wiggle. "It's much nicer to have a fine healthy son. Easier, too. All you want is to have Nicky behave in as fine and strong a way as he looks."

"What I don't understand," said Mrs. Semicolon, "is why Nicky should act in the dreadful way he does. Neither his father nor I have ever bullied *him*."

"Of course you haven't," said Mrs. Piggle-Wiggle. "Neither have I but he acts the same way down here. And, if it is any comfort to you, so did Billy MacIntosh until last week when his mother gave him Bully-baths."

"What in the world are they?" asked Mrs. Semicolon.

"They are just evening baths with a little weakening powder sprinkled in them. With each bath the bully gets weaker and weaker until finally, as in the case of Billy MacIntosh, his two-year-old brother could push him down and sit on him."

"Is he all right now?" asked Mrs. Semicolon.

"Just fine," said Mrs. Piggle-Wiggle.

"How wonderful," said Mrs. Semicolon. "Shall I start the Bullybaths tonight?"

"I was just thinking," said Mrs. Piggle-Wiggle. "In the case of Nicholas I'm not sure the Bullybaths would be the right cure."

"But why?" asked Mrs. Semicolon. "They worked with Billy MacIntosh."

"I know they did," said Mrs. Piggle-Wiggle, "but Billy MacIntosh has little sisters and brothers. No, I think that Nicholas would be better off with Leadership Pills."

"Leadership Pills?" asked Mrs. Semicolon. "What are they?"

"Just little green pills that taste like peppermint," said Mrs. Piggle-Wiggle, "but they bring out wonderful hidden qualities of leadership, especially in only children. Does Nicholas have a playroom or a place where he can bring his friends?"

"Well, he has a very nice bedroom," said Mrs. Semicolon.

"I'm sure he has," said Mrs. Piggle-Wiggle. "But I was thinking more of a place in the cellar or garage or even a tent house in the back yard."

"Oh, I know, I know," said Mrs. Semicolon excitedly. "There is a little old studio out in back. It was built for the artist brother of the people who used to live here. We've used it for garden tools and peat moss and the lawn mower and once Nicholas kept a rabbit there but we could move the garden tools into the cellar and I could have it all fixed up for Nicholas."

Mrs. Piggle-Wiggle said, "Why not let Nicholas fix it up himself?"

"Do you think he could?" asked Mrs. Semicolon.

"Let's wait and see how the Leadership Pills work," said Mrs. Piggle-Wiggle. "If you will send Nicholas over when he comes home from school I'll give him a little bottle to bring home. Give him one pill every day for a week but don't expect miracles. The qualities of leadership are not something you attain overnight. Keep in touch and don't worry."

The very first thing Mrs. Semicolon did after she had hung up the phone was to go out in the yard and look at the old studio. It was late autumn, almost winter and the little old path that led from the back porch past the parsley patch, around the chrysanthemum bed, under the gravenstein apple tree, around the strawberry barrel, past the compost pile to the chestnut tree under which was nestled the old studio, was ankle deep in leaves. They made a nice crumpled newspaper sound as Mrs. Semicolon walked through them. The little old studio needed a coat of paint and the porch was sagging. The front door was hard to open.

Inside was the usual gardener's litter. Spilled peat moss, empty buckets, coffee cans half filled with bone meal and lime. A broken bamboo rake. The power lawn mower. Empty seed packages. Empty flower pots. Nicky's first little bicycle; his last big tricycle; and a Christmas tree stand.

Mrs. Semicolon looked around her and sighed. She wondered if she shouldn't forget what Mrs. Piggle-Wiggle had said and have Old Mac, the handyman, clean the place up. Then she heard the phone ringing and it was Mr. Semicolon wanting to know if she had gotten hold of Mrs. Piggle-Wiggle and what she had said and she had just finished talking to him when Roscoe's mother called to say that the doctor said he was just bruised, and then by the time she had tidied up the house and had a sandwich, it was three-thirty and almost time for Nicky to come home from school.

She fixed a plate of sugar cookies and a glass of milk and a big shiny red apple and put them on the kitchen table. Then she went upstairs and washed her face and combed her hair and put on her grocery store skirt and sweater. She was just finishing her shopping list when she heard a commotion out in the street. She ran to the front window just in time to see Nicky lift his geography book high over his head and bring it down clunk on the skinny little eight year old back of Sylvia Crouch. Quickly Mrs. Semicolon rapped on her window and called out, "Nicky Semicolon, stop that this minute!"

Nicky glanced at his mother then lifted the book up for another blow.

Mrs. Semicolon dashed out of the house, grabbed the book and said, "Aren't you ashamed of yourself? A big boy like you hitting a little girl."

"Well she started it," Nicky said.

"I did not either," Sylvia shrieked. "You took the apple away from my little sister and you pulled my hair."

Mrs. Semicolon said, "Nicholas give Sylvia back her little sister's apple at once."

"I can't," Nicholas said smiling sheepishly. "I ate it."

"All right then," said his mother. "March right into the kitchen and get the apple I put out for you and give it to Sylvia."

Slowly reluctantly Nicholas went in and got the apple. But instead of handing it to Sylvia he threw it at her hard. It hit her in the stomach. "There's your old apple," he said laughing.

Mrs. Semicolon grabbed him by the shoulders and shaking him said, "Nicholas Semicolon, apologize to Sylvia and then go right up to your room at once."

Nicholas not looking at all sorry, said, "Aw, I'm sorry I guess. But I hope your ugly little sister chokes to death on the apple."

Mrs. Semicolon grabbed his arm and hustled him into the house. She was just sending him up to his room when she remembered about Mrs. Piggle-Wiggle and the Leadership Pills. She said, "Go out and get in the car, we're going to the store and then we're going to stop by Mrs. Piggle-Wiggle's for a minute."

In the grocery store Nicholas pushed the basket and Mrs. Semicolon chose the groceries. They got along very well until Mrs. Semicolon left him and the basket up by the dog foods while she went to find the garlic salt. She was on her way back when she heard a child crying. She hurried to where she had left Nicholas and found him pushing his heavy loaded basket as hard as he could into the almost empty basket of a little boy not more than six. The little boy was crying.

Nicholas was laughing and getting ready to give his heavy basket another mighty shove, when a firm hand grabbed him by the collar and sent him spinning into the Mity Pup dog food. One can of Mity Pup hit him on the head. Another landed on his toe. Another cracked him on the wrist. "Ouch," he yelled. "Look out what you're doin'."

"I know what I'm doing," said his mother. "Now stand up and see if you have broken any of that poor little boy's mommie's eggs."

Sulkily Nicholas got to his feet, limped over and opened the box of eggs. Three were cracked. Mrs. Semicolon gave the little boy her box of eggs and took the cracked ones, then she made Nicholas apologize and with his own allowance buy the little boy a box of animal crackers. She didn't let him out of her sight after that, until she got to Mrs. Piggle-Wiggle's house. Then she waited in the car while he went in to get the Leadership Pills.

The yard, the front porch, in fact Mrs. Piggle-Wiggle's whole house was alive with children. They were swinging, digging, sewing, building, painting, singing, teeter-tottering. All busy and happy, until Nicholas opened the gate. The first thing he did was deliberately to bump into and tip over a little boy on a tricycle.

Then he stepped on the fingers of a little girl sitting on the steps playing jacks.

His mother was glad to see that when he came out of the house with the bottle of pills, the little girl who had been playing jacks hit him with a big stick and then ran in the house and slammed the door. Nicholas started after her but his mother honked the horn and shouted at him to come and get in the car.

On the way home she told him how disgracefully he had acted but he only hummed and smiled and acted very unsorry. She gave him one of the Leadership Pills even before she unpacked the groceries, and sent him up to his room to study his geography and think about his loathsome actions. She also told him to take off his brogues and put on his bedroom slippers. He said, "I like these big new shoes. They kick hard."

Well, at dinner that night even though his mother kept looking at him hopefully there was not much evidence of leadership on Nicholas' part unless you can call being the first to the table and eating the most, leadership. However, he didn't step on Josephine's tail and he didn't kick the cat and he did walk quietly in his bedroom slippers.

Mrs. Semicolon was drinking her second cup of coffee when she suddenly remembered poor little Roscoe and the crayons, coloring books and cookies she had promised him. She called Mrs. Eager to see if Roscoe was still awake and when she found he was, she put the things in a basket and was just putting on her coat when Nicholas said, "Let me take the things over, Mother."

Knowing how Mrs. Eager felt about him and also realizing that Mr. Eager who was noted for his violent temper was home, she said, "Are you sure you want to?"

"Yes," said Nicholas in a strange quiet voice. "I'll go change my shoes."

After he had left with the basket Mrs. Semicolon said, "Forthright, I'm worried. I know that it is right that Nicky should take those things to Roscoe and apologize but I'm worried about Hilton Eager. You know what a terrible temper he has. What if he should hit Nicholas?"

"Serve Nicky right," said Mr. Semicolon, unfeelingly.

"I suppose you are right," said Mrs. Semicolon in a worried voice. She cleared the table, washed the dinner dishes, fed the cat, fed Josephine, wrote a note to the milkman, and mended a tear in Nicky's play jacket. Nicky still hadn't come home. She and Mr. Semicolon played a game of cribbage. Mrs. Semicolon usually beat him all to pieces but tonight she was so worried she couldn't count.

Finally Mr. Semicolon said, "Come, come, Carlotta, stop worrying. Nicky's all right."

"But what about Hilton Eager and his terrible temper?"

Just then the front door opened and Nicky came in. He was whistling. His mother called out, "How was Roscoe, Nicky?"

"Oh, he's okay," said Nicky. "We played a couple of games of darts."

"How are his legs?" asked his father.

"They're pretty scratched up," said Nicky. "I'm going to ride him to school on my handle bars tomorrow."

"Did you apologize to him?" asked his mother.

"Yes I did," said Nicky cheerfully. "He was real nice about it but his dad gave me an awful bawling out. For a couple of minutes I thought he was going to sock me . Mrs. Eager wouldn't speak to me at all, at first. But after I apologized she made us some cocoa. She's awful nice. Well, I got two more pages of geography to do. Good night."

Rather self-consciously he kissed his mother and father. Something he hadn't done for weeks. In fact ever since he had become a big swaggering bully.

The next morning at breakfast Mrs. Semicolon gave Nicholas another Leadership Pill. Later she was pleased to see how carefully he helped Roscoe onto the handle bars of his bicycle.

When he came home from school he said, "Say, Mom, these brogues are really too heavy for school. Do you s'pose I could have some new patrol boots?"

"I'll ask your father," she said.

After he had changed into his play clothes his mother asked him where he was going and he said, "I told Sylvia I'd help her patch the tire on her bike."

In about half an hour he was back with Sylvia, her little sister, and Roscoe. Leaving them outside on the porch he came in and whispered excitedly to his mother who was making apple turnovers, "Say, Mom, would you care if I gave my old trike to Sylvia's little sister? Hers is all rusty and anyway it's too little and Sylvia and Roscoe and I are going to paint it up for the baby."

"I think that would be very nice," said Mrs. Semi-colon. "Your old tricycle is out in the garden house. Say, that would be a good place to paint the other tricycle. You could put all that garden stuff down in the cellar."

"Oh, boy," Nicky hugged his mother so hard he got flour in his hair. "By the way," he said as he went out the door, "I asked a boy in my room to come over and play. His name's Jimmy Gopher. He had to go home and ask his mother. Send him out to the garden house when he comes."

Jimmy Gopher, who came streaking up on his bicycle about ten minutes later, was as big and strong and husky as Nicky. He also had red hair and freckles. Mrs. Semicolon was a little worried for fear he and Nicky might not be nice to the smaller children who now included Sylvia, her little sister, her little brother, Roscoe, the Adams twins who were only four and Priscilla Wick who was seven. She kept looking out the kitchen window anxiously but everything seemed to be very peaceful. For a while they all carried things from the garden house to the cellar. Then Sylvia came in for a broom and dustpan. Priscilla Wick wanted a pan of water and a cloth to wash the windows. Jimmy Gopher wanted to know where the turpentine was and Roscoe wanted some steel wool to take the rust off the tricycle.

About four-thirty Mrs. Semicolon put nine apple turnovers on a plate and was about to carry them to the children when she heard a commotion and looked out to see Jimmy Gopher put out his foot and trip Priscilla

who was carrying the pan of water. She fell flat, slopped water all over her play coat and began to cry. Jimmy laughed uproariously. Hurriedly Mrs. Semicolon went to the cupboard and got one of the Leadership Pills. Picking up the plate of turnovers and the pill she opened the back door. She couldn't believe her eyes or her ears. Nicky, her own Nicky, the former bully, was helping Priscilla to her feet and wiping her tears. He was also saying sternly to Jimmy, "Listen, Jim, Priscilla's littler than you and she's a girl. Nobody in our club hits girls or little kids. If you want to hit somebody, hit me *if* you can."

Jimmy said sulkily, "Aw, I didn't hurt her. She's just an old baby."

"I am not," Priscilla said. "I'm the pitcher on the neighborhood baseball team but you got my play coat all wet and I'm going to tell my father and he'll make mashed potatoes out of you."

Sylvia's little sister said "He will, too. He's big."

Mrs. Semicolon said, "How about a hot apple turnover?"

"Hot diggety, Zowie, oh boy," the children cried as they crowded around her.

She gave them each a turnover but before she gave Jimmy his she tucked a Leadership Pill inside the crust.

While the children were eating their little pies, she took Priscilla's coat in and put it on the hall radiator to dry and got one of Nicky's play jackets for her to wear.

There was no more trouble, and just before the children had to go home for dinner Sylvia came excitedly in and asked Mrs. Semicolon to come to the studio and see her little sister's old tricycle which they had painted a beautiful bright red with silver handle bars and silver spokes on the wheels. The old garden house looked beautiful. The windows were shiny clean. The floor was swept and Nicky and Jim had made a table out of two sawhorses and some old boards. "This is our worktable," they told her proudly.

Little Roscoe Eager said, "We got a club, Mrs. Semicolon, and we're all members and it's to fix bicycles and stuff like that."

Priscilla said, "We're going to call it 'The Neighborhood Children's Club.'"

"Nick's the president," Jimmy said, "and I'm the supervisor because I'm awful good at mechanics and fixing things."

"I'm the secretary," Sylvia said. "I'm going to keep notes and make lists of the work we have to do."

"I'm the treasurer," Priscilla said. "I collect the dues and take the money when we sell lemonade and stuff like that."

"I'm the salesman," Roscoe said. "I go around and find work for us to do."

"We're the helpers," said the Adams twins and Sylvia's little sister. "We run home and get Daddy's hammer."

"Well, I'll be in charge of refreshments," said Mrs. Semicolon.

"And so will I," said Mrs. Eager who had come over to find Roscoe and had been standing on the stoop listening. "I think The Neighborhood Children's Club is such a wonderful idea I'm going to bake brownies for tomorrow's meeting."

"And," said Mrs. Semicolon, "I'm going to scout around and see if I can't find some furniture for the clubhouse. I'm sure I've got an old kitchen table and four chairs up in the attic."

"And, Mom, would you care if we had a fire in the fireplace on cold days," Nicky asked, "if we put up a firescreen and were very very careful?"

"I have an old grate they can have," said Mrs. Eager. "And if they burn coal and use the firescreen I think it would be quite safe, don't you, Carlotta?"

"Nick and I'll watch out for the little kids," said Jimmy earnestly. "After all we're the oldest and biggest."

Well, The Neighborhood Children's Club grew and grew. Different mothers gave them furniture—they even had an old couch—and some dishes and cookies and apples and cider and peanuts and popcorn. Mr. Semicolon built the boys a fine tool bench and gave them some of his older tools. Even Mr. Eager, who was a very good carpenter, controlled his terrible temper and came over and helped them build a porch. The Adams twins' mother, who used to be an artist, painted them a beautiful sign with smiling little children holding up red letters that spelled out "The Neighborhood Children's Club."

The day they put up the sign they invited Mrs. Piggle-Wiggle over for tea. Mrs. Semicolon had made a coconut cake and Mrs. Eager brought over a big plate of fudge. There was a nice fire in the fireplace and pink-and-white-checked tablecloth on the old kitchen table which Sylvia and Priscilla had painted pink. The only trouble was that the paint wasn't dry and the tablecloth stuck, in fact they never could get it off, but it certainly looked pretty that day.

Just before she went home Mrs. Piggle-Wiggle went in to see Mrs. Semicolon. Mrs. Semicolon said, "Oh, Mrs. Piggle-Wiggle I'll never be able to thank you. Never."

Mrs. Piggle-Wiggle said, "Don't thank me. Thank Mr. Piggle-Wiggle for leaving me that old sea chest full of magic cures for children. It was one of the finest things he ever did."

"Oh, by the way," said Mrs. Semicolon, "I have quite a few Leadership Pills left. Let me get them for you."

"Why don't you just keep them," said Mrs. Piggle-Wiggle. "I have lots more and with new children moving into the neighborhood and a clubhouse in your back yard, they might come in very handy."

"Well, I have used them on two of the older children, I mean besides Nicky," said Mrs. Semicolon. "Oh, Mrs. Piggle-Wiggle, I'm very proud of Nicky. He's so patient and kind to the little children."

"Of course he is," said Mrs. Piggle-Wiggle. "Down inside he probably always was. It is just that sometimes with children, especially boys, their bodies grow faster than their patience and kindness. All Leadership Pills do is even things up. Of course having that wonderful clubhouse helps a lot. Busy children are happy children, and happy children are seldom quarrelsome."

As Mrs. Piggle-Wiggle walked off down the street

in the dusk, her dog Wag on one side, Lightfoot the cat on the other, Mrs. Semicolon wiped her eyes with a corner of her apron and said to nobody in particular, "There goes the most wonderful little person in the whole world."

IV. THE WHISPERER

ON FRIDAY AFTERNOONS Miss Weathervane read to the fourth-grade class. She usually read for about half an hour but if the story was very interesting and the children were quiet and well behaved she often read longer. This Friday she was reading from a book of Japanese folk tales, a story called "The Man Who Bought a Dream."

As she was reading "Sssssssssssss, ssssss, Teeheeeeeheeee," came from the far corner of the schoolroom. Miss Weathervane stopped reading. She said, "When Evelyn Rover and Mary Crackle stop whispering I shall continue."

But Evelyn and Mary were so busy whispering they didn't hear her. Their desks were opposite each other and by leaning across the aisle they could put their heads together and whisper and giggle very conveniently. They were whispering about Evelyn's birthday party which was next Saturday and how Evelyn's mother had told her to invite every little girl in her class but she just wouldn't ask that awful old Cornelia Whitehouse who lived in a trailer and got her clothes from the St. Vincent de Paul rummage sale. "Ssssssssssss, sssssssssss, teeheeheeteeheehee," they hissed and giggled while the class waited impatiently for Miss

Weathervane to go on with the story.

Finally Miss Weathervane put her pencil in the book to hold the place, stood up, rapped on the desk with her ruler and said in a loud clear voice, "EVELYN ROVER AND MARY CRACKLE! COME TO THE FRONT OF THE ROOM AT ONCE!"

The two little girls jumped guiltily, then stood up and walked up to Miss Weathervane's desk. Mary was embarrassed and a little bit frightened. But Evelyn tossed her pony tail which was held with two "sterling silver" barrettes, shuffled her party shoes which she wore to school every day and lowered her eyelids in an attempt to look superior and bored. Mary who was her very best friend and admired everything she did, wished she could be like Evelyn and not be scared of her teacher and look haughty like a princess.

Miss Weathervane said, "I'm sure the class would appreciate it if you girls would tell us all what is so important that it can't wait until after story time."

Mary blushed and hung her head.

Evelyn said boldly, "I'd like to tell you Miss Weathervane, I really would, but I promised my mama I wouldn't because it's about my birthday party and everybody isn't invited." She turned around and looked meaningly at poor little Cornelia Whitehouse then at Mary, who simpered.

Miss Weathervane said sharply, "As long as the party is not school business I would prefer that you did not discuss it during school hours, *especially* when I am reading. Also I would like to have you both stay after school and write a report on the stories we have read this afternoon. Now take your seats."

Mary slunk to the back of the room and sat down. She didn't look at any of her classmates. But Evelyn looked triumphantly around the room then slowly sauntered back to her seat. Her pony tail switched impudently behind her. After she had sat down, she banged open her desk and made as much noise as she could getting out a pencil and some paper for her book report. Mary watched her admiringly and giggled behind her hand.

Miss Weathervane sighed. She opened up the book and went on with the story. She looked up at the class.

They were all smiling happily. Especially Cornelia Whitehouse whose pale cheeks were flushed and her eyes shining with joy.

"You enjoyed the story, didn't you, Cornelia?" asked Miss Weathervane gently.

"Oh, yes," said Cornelia sighing. "It was just wonderful."

From the back of the room came the squeaky twitter of giggles followed by the snakelike hiss of whispering. Mary and Evelyn had their heads together again, their hands cupped by the mouths, their eyes on Cornelia. Miss Weathervane said sharply, "Class dismissed, all except Mary and Evelyn."

When Mary and Evelyn finally finished their reports and brought them up to the teacher's desk, Miss Weathervane said, "Have you girls ever thought how you would feel if you had no father and no pretty clothes? Especially if two of your classmates whose fathers had fine positions, whispered about you and giggled and didn't invite you to their birthday parties?"

Mary hung her head and picked at the buttons on her sweater.

Evelyn said, "I wouldn't care."

"But you would," Miss Weathervane said. "You'd care more than anyone in this class because you are a vain little girl and clothes are very important to you."

"My mama says I have natural style," Evelyn said. "She says I'm going to be a fashion model when I grow up."

Mary said, "Me, too."

Evelyn laughed condescendingly. "Oh, Mary, don't

be silly," she said. "You couldn't be a model, you're too fat."

Miss Weathervane said, "Some day you will learn, Evelyn, that a kind heart and humility are more important to beauty than a 'natural style.' Now run along both of you. I have papers to correct."

All the way home from school Evelyn and Mary giggled and whispered about Cornelia and her raggy old clothes, Miss Weathervane and how mad they had made her, the party, boys, and how Karen Elroyd always wanted to play post office, wasn't that awful? When they got to Mary's house which was next door to Evelyn's, a big black cloud slid suddenly over the sun and large drops of rain began to splat onto the sidewalks. "Ooooooooeeeeeee," they squealed and pulled their school coats up over their heads. Mary's mother who was on her knees by the fence weeding her perennial bed, called out, "Hi, girls, how was school?"

"Oh, it was okay," Mary said, then cupping her hand in front of her mouth she whispered to Evelyn, "Don't tell her about staying after school."

"I won't," whispered Evelyn.

"Whispering's rude," remarked Mary's mother conversationally from behind a clump of phlox.

"Gollee, your mama sounds mad," whispered Evelyn behind her hand to Mary.

"Oh, she's not mad," whispered back Mary. "She just doesn't like whispering."

"Sssssssss, sssssss, ssssssss," said Mary's mother wiping her hands on her blue jeans. "You sound like a couple of old snakes. Maybe I'd better go downtown and buy some snakefood and throw away that fresh chocolate cake I have for you in the kitchen."

"Chocolate cake!" shrieked the little girls. "Goody. That's neat." They ran into the house and slammed the back door. Mrs. Crackle went on weeding, in spite of the raindrops which were coming down faster and faster. By the time she had finished the perennial bed her hair was soaked, rain was running into her eyes. But Mary's mother smiled happily. It was a warm spring rain and would be wonderful for the garden. She put the hoe on top of the weeds and trowel in the wheelbarrow and was just going to push it into the garage when she noticed a forlorn little figure leaning on the gate. She said, "Hello, there. Are you one of Mary's little friends?"

Cornelia Whitehouse, for that was who it was, said, "Well, I'm in Mary's room at school. My, you have a pretty yard. I just love gardens. We live in a trailer and can't have one."

Mary's mother said, "Then your daddy must work in the big factory."

"Not my daddy, he's dead," the little girl said. "My mom works there. One of the ladies at the plant who works with Mom owns the trailer and lets us live there."

"Oh, my goodness, what's the matter with me?" said Mary's mother. "Here we are standing out in the rain and getting all wet. Let's go in the house. Mary and her little friend Evelyn are in the kitchen eating chocolate cake I just baked." She walked over and pushed open the gate but the little girl hung back.

"Hurry," said Mary's mother pushing the gate open

wider. A big gust of wind came whooshing around the house and the rain came down even faster. Still the little girl hung back. Mary's mother reached out and took her hand and pulled her into the yard. "Come along," she said smiling. "Let's hurry before those little pigs eat up all the cake." Pulling Cornelia along with her she ran up the path, on to the back porch and into the kitchen.

"Look," she said to Mary and Evelyn who were sitting at the kitchen table eating large wedges of chocolate cake, "I've brought a little friend for you."

"Where'd you find *her?*" Mary asked ungraciously.

"She came sailing in on a big gust of wind," her mother said.

Mary and Evelyn gave each other sly looks, put their heads together and began to whisper.

Mrs. Crackle said sharply, "Mary, where are your manners? Introduce your little friend and invite her to have some cake."

Mary looked at Evelyn who cupped her hand over her mouth, leaned over and whispered something in Mary's ear. Mary giggled. Evelyn giggled. Cornelia flushed.

Mrs. Crackle said, "MARY CRACKLE STOP THAT WHISPERING THIS INSTANT. It is rude and unkind and I won't have it. Now Mary stand up and greet your little friend and introduce her."

Slowly, sulkily Mary stood up, and said, "Mother I'd like you to meet Cornelia ... uh ... uh ..."

"Ragbag," said Evelyn in a loud whisper. Both girls burst into giggles.

Mrs. Crackle said, "Mary, go up to your room and stay there! Evelyn you may go home. Cornelia let's you and me have a cup of tea and a piece of cake."

"Oh, that's all right," said Cornelia in a very low voice. "I better go."

"You'll do no such thing," said Mrs. Crackle. "Hurry up, Mary, go up to your room. Here's your coat, Evelyn, now scat."

Mary said, "But Evelyn hasn't finished her cake, I think it's rude to send her home before she finishes."

"I'll handle the manners in this family," said her mother. "Now you march."

Mary went sulkily out of the kitchen and Evelyn slammed the door hard as she went out. Mrs. Crackle cut two hunks of the fresh gooey chocolate cake, poured boiling water in the teapot and then she and Cornelia sat down. As they ate she asked Cornelia about school and her trailer house and if she had any little girls to play with which she hadn't and Cornelia asked her about flowers and how to grow them and how long it took for them to bloom.

They were just finishing their tea party when there was a knock at the back door and it was Evelyn who said that her mother had sent her over to apologize which she did very ungraciously and then she said, "Cornelia, Mama says I *have* to invite you to my birthday party. It is a week from tomorrow at twelve o'clock."

"Oh, thank you," said Cornelia smiling. "Thank you Evelyn, ever so much for asking me."

Evelyn did not smile back. She opened the back door, started out, then turned and said, "Try and wear a clean dress if you have one." She slammed the door and was gone.

Cornelia's face turned very red and two big tears splashed down on to the crumbs on her plate. Mary's mother said, "It's sometimes very hard for me to remember what a nice little girl Evelyn used to be. Now, I've got an idea about the party. I think it is a pretty good one but if you don't like it you just say so. This is it. We both like gardening and I have a big garden and need help with the weeding and transplanting, so, why don't you come here after school every day and help me in the garden and for payment I'll get you a new dress to wear to Evelyn's party."

Cornelia said, "Oh boy! I'll come tomorrow right after school. I'll run all the way."

"That won't be necessary," Mary's mother said laughing. "But you had better bring along some old jeans and shoes—weeding is pretty dirty work. Now as soon as I put these dishes in the sink I'll drive you home."

Cornelia said, "I'll clear up the dishes, Mrs. Crackle. I'd like to." She jumped to her feet and began carrying the plates and cups to the sink.

Mary's mother said, "Thank you very much, Cornelia. I'd appreciate that. I'll just run up and get out of my gardening clothes, then I'll drive you home."

After she had changed her clothes Mrs. Crackle went into Mary's room and asked Mary, who was sitting glumly by the window looking out at the rain, if she wouldn't like to go with her when she drove Cornelia home.

Mary said, "Can Evelyn come, too?"

"No she can't," said Mrs. Crackle crisply. "She was very rude to Cornelia this afternoon and anyway I can't bear her silly giggling and whispering."

Mary said, "Evelyn Rover is my very very best friend in all the world and I love everything about her and if you don't want her along then I don't want to go. What did Cornelia have to come over here for anyway? Nobody likes her."

Mrs. Crackle said, "She is lonely. Her mother works and when she comes home from school she comes home to a little empty trailer in a shabby miserable little trailer park. How would you like to live like that?"

"I wouldn't," Mary said. "I think it's awful and I'm sorry for her and I'm ashamed I said anything about her clothes."

"Of course you are," Mary's mother said putting her arm around her. "Now run in and wash your face and hurry because it's getting late and I have to go to the store."

When they got downstairs Cornelia had finished the dishes and was rinsing out the dog's water dish. Mrs. Crackle thanked her and Mary said, "Gosh, everything looks neat, Cornelia. I wish you'd come over every afternoon."

"She's going to for a while," said Mrs. Crackle. "She's going to help me in the garden."

Mary looked surprised but before she could say anything Robby and Billy, her two little brothers, came crashing in the back door. Robby was carrying a baby robin and Billy a part of an old nest. Robby said, "Mom, look at the poor little robin. We found him lying on the sidewalk right in front of Armstrong's and I bet their old cat knocked him down."

Billy said, "His poor little old nest was lying right beside him and there was an eggshell in it. Do you think if we fixed the nest up and put it in our room he'd stay in it?"

"I'm sure I don't know," said Mrs. Crackle. "Let me see the bird." Gently she took the baby bird from Robby and put him down on the kitchen table. He slumped down and put his head under his wing. Mrs. Crackle said, "I wonder what's the matter. Frankly I don't know much about baby birds."

"I do," said Cornelia. "I had a baby robin last year. I think this little bird's hungry. You boys go out and dig him some angleworms and I'll fix him a box, just the way I did for my bird."

"Where do you find angleworms?" Robby asked.

"In the compost pile out by the garage. There are lots of angleworms out there," said Mrs. Crackle.

"How do you feed birds?" Mary asked.

"As soon as the boys get the worms I'll show you," Cornelia said. "But first we have to fix a box. We need an old shoe box and some cotton."

Mrs. Crackle said, "There's a shoe box on the shelf of my closet, and a roll of cotton in the top drawer of the linen closet. Mary, you run up and get them."

Mary put her hand over her mouth and whispered to

Cornelia, "Come on up with me and I'll show you my charm bracelet. I have a little silver telephone with a receiver that really comes off the hook."

Cornelia cupped her hand over her mouth and whispered back, "Tomorrow when I come over, I'll bring my pictures of movie stars. I've got over a hundred."

Mary whispered, "Over a hundred! How neat! Bring them for sure."

"Sssssssssss, ssssss, sssssss," said Mrs. Crackle. "Here come the boys and you haven't fixed the nest."

Mary and Cornelia ran upstairs and Cornelia had the box fixed in just a jiffy. When they came downstairs Robby and Billy were standing by the bird whom they had named Admiral after Admiral Byrd, trying to get him to take his head out from under his wing and eat a fat nervous worm that was thrashing around on the kitchen table.

Cornelia cupped her hand over her mouth and whispered to Mary, "Aren't boys dumb? They don't even know how to feed a bird?"

Mary giggled "Teheeteeheeteehee." And whispered, "Boys are dumb and worms are disgusting. Ugh!"

Robby and Billy said, "Aw, quit your whispering and giggling and show us how to feed the bird."

Cornelia walked over to the table and picked up the worm.

Mary squealed, "Eeeeeeeek, don't touch him Cornelia."

Cornelia said, "He's just an old angleworm. Here," she picked up the worm and began tickling Admiral with it. After a little bit the robin lifted up his head,

saw the worm, opened his mouth and Cornelia dropped the worm in. He gulped a few times then opened his mouth for more. This time Robby dropped the worm in. Then Billy. Then Cornelia, then Robby, then Billy. And finally Mary.

Then Mrs. Crackle said that she just had to go to the store and did the boys want to come or stay and dig worms for their bird. They, of course, elected to stay home and feed the bird and so Cornelia and Mary and Mrs. Crackle went to the store and drove Cornelia home.

When Mary saw the ugly old unpainted trailer with the trash-littered yard where Cornelia lived she felt very ashamed of the way she and Evelyn had acted. Impulsively she whispered to Cornelia, "How would you like to be in Evelyn's and my secret society? We call it the Hush Hush Club."

"Oh, I'd just love it," Cornelia whispered back.

"I'll see you at school tomorrow morning, then," whispered Mary.

"Okay," Cornelia whispered. And she was so used to whispering that she whispered, "Thank you for the cake and for taking me home," to Mrs. Crackle and then they all laughed and Mrs. Crackle said, "You girls had better watch out you might forget how to speak out loud."

On the way home Mary told her mother how sorry she felt for Cornelia and how she had asked her to be a member of the Hush Hush Club. Mrs. Crackle told Mary about Evelyn's party and how hateful Evelyn had been and how she had asked Cornelia to help her in the garden in exchange for a new party dress. Mary said that she thought her mother was just wonderful and leaned over and hugged her.

Mrs. Crackle smiled happily to herself because, even though Mary hadn't stopped whispering, she certainly was being her own sweet friendly self again and Mrs. Crackle could hardly wait to tell Mr. Crackle.

The next morning was beautiful with sunshine and birds singing and Admiral Byrd still alive and peeping. Right after breakfast Evelyn knocked at the back door. She was wearing a new green dress with a huge full skirt, new green slippers, a new green sweater and she had a green ribbon tied around her pony tail.

Mary said, "Oh, Evelyn you look adorable. Just adorable."

Evelyn blinked her eyes and said, "Oh, I don't think so."

Mary's mother said, "Don't forget your spelling book, Mary, and remember you're going to walk home with Cornelia tonight."

Evelyn said, "Cornelia! That ragbag. How come?"

Mary cupped her hand around her mouth and whispered, "I feel awfully sorry for her, she lives in a dumpy old trailer and she's going to help Mother in the garden."

Evelyn cupped her hand around her mouth and whispered, "I don't feel sorry for her. I think she's goopy. Her clothes are dirty. I'm just furious Mama made me ask her to my party."

Mr. Crackle said crossly, "Sssssss, sssss, sssssss. The two little town gossips . . ."

Mary said, "Oh, Daddy! Come on, Evelyn we have to hurry." She whispered to her again, "Ssssssss. Sssssss. Ssssss."

"Oh, go on to school," said Mrs. Crackle crossly. "I'm sick to death of your whispering and giggling."

After the little girls had gone she poured Mr. Crackle and herself another cup of coffee. As he stirred sugar into his cup Mr. Crackle said, "Something has to be done about those two dreadful little females."

"But what?" asked Mrs. Crackle. "What would you suggest?"

"I guess we'd better call Mrs. Piggle-Wiggle," said Mr. Crackle.

"I guess we'd better," said Mrs. Crackle. "And right now."

But of course she didn't get to call Mrs. Piggle-Wiggle "right now" because Robby and Billy had to leave for school while Admiral was still hungry, so Mrs. Crackle spent the entire morning digging in her compost pile for angleworms. By the time she finally got Admiral filled up she was so tired she had to sit down and have a cup of coffee. Then she had to wash the breakfast dishes and make the beds and dust the living room.

She was just finishing when Mrs. Rover knocked at the door and to Mrs. Crackle's surprise said, "Elizabeth, I'm worried to death about Evelyn. She's gotten so mean lately. She whispers and gossips all the time and I was just shocked when she told me she hadn't invited that poor little Cornelia to her party. She never speaks in a normal tone of voice any more. It's sssss,

sssss, from morning till night. Carter and I are nearly frantic."

Mrs. Crackle said, "It's just as bad over here if that is any comfort to you. In fact Cantilever calls Evelyn and Mary the Town Gossips. He wants me to telephone Mrs. Piggle-Wiggle. I was just about to when you called."

"You mean that funny little woman who lives down on Vinemaple?"

"Yes, that's Mrs. Piggle-Wiggle and she knows more about children than anybody in town and she has all sorts of magic cures for their bad habits."

"Well, for heavens sake let's call her right away," said Evelyn's mother. "Maybe she can tell us how to get rid of Mary and Evelyn's meanness before the party. If she can't I do declare I don't think I'll have the party."

When Mrs. Piggle-Wiggle heard about Evelyn and Mary she said, "There must be an epidemic of whispering going around. I'm almost out of Whisper Sticks."

"Whisper Sticks?" asked Mrs. Crackle. "What are they?"

"They're magic candy sticks," said Mrs. Piggle-Wiggle. "Two or three sucks and you can't speak above a whisper. Also, they have a very nice flavor—sort of raspberry cherry and children love them, especially little girls."

"How long does this not speaking above a whisper last?" asked Mary's mother.

"Usually all day," said Mrs. Piggle-Wiggle. "Depends upon how fast the child eats the Whisper Stick.

How many do you think you and Mrs. Rover will need?"

"I really don't know," said Mary's mother. "What do you think?"

"I should say seven," said Mrs. Piggle-Wiggle promptly. "Three each for Evelyn and Mary, and one for Cornelia."

"But Cornelia doesn't need any," exclaimed Mrs. Crackle.

"She will," said Mrs. Piggle-Wiggle. "As soon as she gets friendly with Mary she'll start whispering, they always do. I'll send the Whisper Sticks home with Billy and Robby, they have a Cub Scout meeting here today."

"Oh, thank you so much, Mrs. Piggle-Wiggle," said Mary's mother gratefully.

"No trouble at all," said Mrs. Piggle-Wiggle. "Please call and let me know how everything turns out."

"Oh, I will," said Mary's mother.

Then she told Evelyn's mother all about the Whisper Sticks and she was delighted, in fact they were both so happy and talked so much about the wonderful cure they began to think it had already happened. It was a great disappointment to them when Evelyn and Mary came walking up the street their arms around each other's waists, their heads together, whispering for all they were worth while behind them looking forlorn and friendless sagged Cornelia.

"Just look at that," said Evelyn's mother stirring her coffee angrily. "Those two hateful little old things with their heads together sayin' mean things about that poor little Cornelia."

"Of course we don't know that they are," said Mary's mother passing the cake. "But it certainly looks that way. However, Cornelia came over to help me with the garden so the way Mary and Evelyn treat her doesn't make much difference today. If you'll pardon me just a minute I'll go out and get her started. I do hope she brought her jeans."

Jumping to her feet Evelyn's mother said, "I'm going right home and make that poor little thing a ham sandwich. She's nothing but a bundle of little bones."

Mary's mother said, "Make her a peanut butter sandwich right here. Pour a glass of milk and cut her a big piece of cake, too, will you? I'll go out and bring her in."

Stepping outside, Mary's mother called, "Cornelia. May I speak to you?"

Instantly Evelyn and Mary who had separated for a minute, put their heads together and began Ssssssss, ssssssssssing again.

Briskly Mrs. Crackle said, "You too, Mary. Come here I want to speak to you."

Cornelia came running but Mary and Evelyn parted slowly like two sticky caramels being pulled apart, gave each other long meaningful looks, then doubled up in giggles. When Mary finally started up the back steps, Mrs. Crackle couldn't help giving her a hard little spank.

"Hey, that hurt," Mary said, looking surprised.

"I meant it to," said Mrs. Crackle. "It's to remind

you that you and Evelyn were rude and hateful just now. Go upstairs and change your clothes and lend Cornelia a tee shirt. She forgot to bring one."

Cornelia had forgotten a tee shirt but she hadn't forgotten her scrapbook of movie stars. She and Mary whispered and giggled over it upstairs while they were changing their clothes and downstairs while they were eating their sandwiches and cake. Then while Cornelia pulled weeds Mary sat in the wheelbarrow and looked at the pictures and she and Cornelia giggled and whispered about them.

After a while Evelyn came over to see what they were doing but Mary wouldn't show her the book and she and Cornelia whispered and giggled so rudely that finally Evelyn yelled out, "Oh, you make me sick, old fatty and ragbag. I hate you both!"

"Sticks and stones may break my bones but names will never hurt me," chanted Cornelia as she deftly pulled the grass from around the delphiniums.

Mrs. Crackle and Mrs. Rover watching the children from the breakfast-room window, were ashamed to see how hateful they were acting. Then Mary had to go to her music lesson and when she had gone Evelyn came over and she and Cornelia giggled and whispered over the book of movie stars.

Mrs. Crackle and Mrs. Rover thought that Billy and Robby would never get there with those Whisper Sticks. But they did, finally and as soon as they had changed their clothes and taken Admiral out to the compost pile for his afternoon snack of about a hundred worms, Mrs. Crackle gave Evelyn and Cornelia each a Whisper Stick. "Oh, thank you very much," both girls said as they quickly peeled off the paper.

"Um, this candy *is* good," said Cornelia happily licking her stick. "What kind is it?"

"I'm not sure who makes the candy," said Mrs. Crackle, "but I've been told it is delicious."

"Oh, it is," said Evelyn biting off a chunk. "It is sssssssssssssssssss."

Mrs. Crackle couldn't hear the rest of what she said because her voice disappeared and she spoke in a faint whisper, like tissue paper in a Christmas box.

"What did you say, Evelyn?" asked Cornelia. Her voice had grown low and very quiet. A perfect library voice.

"Speak louder, Cornelia, I can't hear you," Evelyn said, but nobody could hear her because her words came out a soft whish like the rustle of a silk petticoat.

"What did you say?" Cornelia asked, but Evelyn couldn't hear her because her voice was now the soft crooning of a mother putting a baby to sleep.

Then Mary came home from her music lesson. "Hi Evelyn, hi Cornelia," she called out happily.

"Sssssssss, sssssss," said Evelyn. She sounded like the wind blowing through prairie grass.

"Sssssss, sssssss," called out Cornelia, who now sounded like the tiny singing of a teakettle.

"If you kids are going to whisper about me I'm going in the house," Mary said angrily.

Mrs. Crackle said, "How about a stick of candy?"

"I'd love one," said Mary. "I'm starving."

Her mother gave her a stick of the candy and she

eagerly pulled down the waxed paper and began suck-
ing.

After about three sucks she turned to her mother and
said, "Miss Prince says that I can have two new pieces
next time." She looked happy but she gasped out her
words as if she had been running for about a hundred
miles.

"That's fine dear," said Mrs. Crackle. "Perhaps she
will let you try 'The Witches Dance.'"

"Oh, I hope so," said Mary, or rather buzzed Mary,
because now she sounded like a bee on a screen door.

Cornelia on her knees in the delphinium bed, sat
back on her heels and said, "I'm almost through here,
Mrs. Crackle, what do you want me to do next?"

Mrs. Crackle didn't answer her, in fact didn't even
look at her, because all she could hear was a thin little
hissing sound like a leak in the hose. Cornelia repeated
what she had said, this time shouting as loud as she
could. This time she sounded like dried peas rattling
in their pods.

Mary, seeing that Cornelia was talking and not being
able to hear her, of course, decided that she was whispering to Evelyn. Angrily biting off a piece of her
candy stick Mary said, "I told you kids that if you
didn't stop whispering I would go in the house, and I
mean it."

Of course Evelyn and Cornelia didn't pay any attention to her because all they could hear was a thin little
noise like a faraway broom sweeping a faraway floor.
Evelyn said, "As soon as Cornelia finishes her gardening let's go over to my house and make caramel apples

—Mama lets me make them any time I want."

She waited for excited squeals but Cornelia, who was gazing up at Mrs. Crackle waiting for instructions, didn't even turn her head. Mary who was stamping angrily toward the house didn't turn around and Mrs. Crackle who was grown up and should have had good manners walked into the house behind Mary. Of course nobody heard her, for who can hear a spring breeze riffling through the apple blossoms?

Evelyn flounced out of the wheelbarrow, slammed down Cornelia's movie star book, stamped out of the yard and slammed the gate. Then she called back, "I hate you all! You are all rude and horrible and mean and if you come to my birthday party, I'll stamp on your presents and slam the door in your faces."

Cornelia who hadn't seen Evelyn go and had gone back to her weeding looked up and seeing nobody said to herself, "That's funny. I heard a little noise like somebody brushing sugar off a shelf. But there is nobody around so it must have been the trees." She took another suck of her candy stick, wrapped it up and put it in her pocket, and went on with her weeding.

In a few minutes Mary came out and sat down in the wheelbarrow. She said, "I thought you were my friend. How come you were whispering to Evelyn?"

Cornelia said, "You're whispering too softly, I can't hear you."

Mary said, "I can see your lips move but no words come out. What's the matter?"

"What did you say?" Cornelia asked.

"I said, 'I CAN SEE YOUR LIPS MOVE BUT

NO WORDS COME OUT! WHAT'S THE MAT-
TER?' " Mary shouted.

Cornelia said, "Why do you whisper? Nobody is
around to hear us."

"I'M NOT WHISPERING!" Mary screamed.

"Stop whispering!" Cornelia said.

"I CAN'T HEAR YOU!" Mary yelled. "TALK
LOUDER."

"I'M TALKING AS LOUD AS I CAN. IN
FACT I'M SCREAMING," screamed Cornelia.

Then because Cornelia had put her candy away
while she was weeding and hadn't had a lick for quite
a while, her voice began to come back a tiny bit. In
fact Mary could make out, "I'm screaming."

She said angrily, "You are not screaming. You're whispering as softly as you can. I think you're mean. I got you into the Hush Hush Club and now you're whispering about me."

As far as Cornelia was concerned all that was coming out of Mary's mouth were faint little gasping breaths. She had no idea what she was saying or trying to say. In fact she thought Mary was teasing her and pretending to talk the way the members of the Hush Hush Club did to nonmembers. Furiously she said, "Okay then, be mean, I don't care. Anyway I'm going in the house to talk to your mother."

She got up and ran into the house.

Then Evelyn who had been sitting on her front steps sulking and licking her Whisper Stick, saw Mary alone and called out, "Hey, Mary, come on over. I'm going to make caramel apples."

Of course Mary couldn't hear her any more than she could hear the leaves rubbing against each other in the chestnut tree at the end of the block. But Evelyn who had no idea that she was whispering because her voice sounded perfectly normal to her ears, thought Mary didn't answer because she was mad at her. She began to cry. Her tears made big wet marks on her new green dress and new green slippers. She didn't care. She was lonely and unhappy.

So was Mary who was still standing by the wheelbarrow.

Then Corinthian Bop, the most popular boy in their room, came wheeling around the corner on his bicycle. Evelyn quickly wiped away her tears, straightened out her skirt and called out, "Hi, Corry!"

Corinthian looked at her but as he couldn't hear anything, he rode right on by muttering, "Stuck-up old thing." Then he saw Mary.

She smiled and said, "Hi, Corry, want to see our baby bird?"

Naturally he couldn't hear her, but as she had smiled he stopped, got off his bike, leaned it against the fence and sauntered into the yard. "Whatcha doing?" he asked Mary.

"Oh, nothing," she said, but as he couldn't hear her he said louder, "I SAID WHATCHA DOING?" Mary said, "Want to see our baby robin? His name's Admiral Byrd and he's adorable but he eats worms, ugh."

Corinthian said, "What are you whisperin' for? Your silly old girl friends aren't around."

Mary said, "I'm not whispering. I'm talking in a perfectly normal tone of voice."

Turning and walking out of the yard, Corinthian said, "Aw you make me sick."

"I don't know what's the matter with you," Mary said. "I'm not whispering. I'M NOT."

"Don't talk if you don't want to," Corinthian said as he got on his bike. "You don't have anything to say anyway." He rode away.

Mary began to cry. Cornelia came out of the house and began weeding the flower bed by the porch. Mary walked over to her and said, "What's the matter with me? Nobody can hear what I say." Then she had an idea. She rushed into the house and got a pencil and a pad of paper. On it she wrote, "Something is the matter with my throat. Nobody can hear what I say. Call the doctor." She took this note in to her mother who, with Mrs. Rover, was going through fashion books looking for a dress for Cornelia.

Mrs. Crackle read the note and said, "There's nothing wrong with your throat, Mary. It is just that you have been whispering so much lately your vocal cords have decided that you didn't like them and have taken a little vacation."

"But when will they be back?" wrote Mary.

"When you stop whispering," said her mother. "I imagine that if you took a pledge to stop whispering entirely, except on very necessary occasions such as speaking in the library and telling nice secrets about birthday presents and things like that, your voice would be back at work tomorrow morning."

"What about Cornelia and Evelyn?" wrote Mary. "They whisper all the time."

"They are suffering from the same disease you are," said Mrs. Crackle. "Now I'll tell you what to do. You go and tell or rather write down what I have said and show it to Cornelia and Evelyn. Then you write out a pledge giving a solemn oath that you promise never to gossip and to whisper except when absolutely necessary."

"But Mother," Mary scribbled excitedly, "how can we have the Hush Hush Club if we don't whisper? That was the main purpose of the club. Everything was secret."

"Then I think it is high time it was broken up," said

her mother. "I don't approve of little whispering secret groups. Perhaps you can think of a better kind of club to organize."

"What about a Picnic Club?" asked Evelyn's mother. "You could go on picnics every Saturday and we mothers would provide the lunches."

"That would be fun," said Mrs. Crackle. "And on rainy days you could write plays and act in them."

Mary thought for a minute or two then wrote, "I'll have to see what the other members think."

Her mother said, "Well, write a note to the two that are here now and tell them to come in here I want to talk to them. And," she added, winking at Mrs. Rover, "I wouldn't eat any more of that candy stick if I were you. Candy is very very hard on tired vocal cords. Tell the other girls that, too."

After Mary had gone out to get Evelyn and Cornelia, Mrs. Rover said to Mrs. Crackle, "You know, Elizabeth, I do believe that those children have learned a lesson. I don't think we're going to have to use the rest of those Whisper Sticks. You'd better send them back to Mrs. Piggle-Wiggle."

"Better yet, I'm going to give them to Miss Weathervane," said Mary's mother. "She told me that the whispering during Friday story time had gotten so bad she had almost decided to give up reading to the children altogether. I'm going to tell her to break the Whisper Sticks up into little pieces and give each whisperer one before the reading starts."

"What a wonderful idea," said Mrs. Rover, "and you know what, Elizabeth, I'm going to take one Whisper Stick and keep it on hand just in case any whispering breaks out at the party. Oh, that party is going to be a big success now! I can hardly wait. But don't you really think that pink would be better for Cornelia, she is so pale."

"Whatever you say," said Mary's mother. "You're the one who knows about fashion. Now I had better call Mrs. Piggle-Wiggle and thank her."

V. THE SLOWPOKE

"HARBIN!" called Mrs. Quadrangle. "Breakfast! I'm making waffles, so hurry, dear."

"Coming, Mom," Harbin answered. But unless "coming" means sitting on the bed in your underwear watching a beetle crawling on the screen, Harbin wasn't.

After he had watched the beetle for five or ten minutes, Harbin slowly reached out and picked up a sock. He looked at the sock fixedly almost as if he were waiting for it to say something to him, then let it slide out of his fingers. It fell across his shoe. He lay back on his bed, folded his arms behind his head and gazed up at the ceiling. There was a brown stain just over his head where the roof had leaked the winter they had the hurricane. The stain looked just like a map of South America. Harbin was trying to figure out where the Amazon River and those little fish that ate a man right down to his skeleton in three minutes were when his mother called again, "Haaaaaaaaaaaarbin! Breakfast!"

"Coming, Mom," he answered. The spot really looked more like Africa he decided. Boy, he'd sure like to go to Africa! He bet that if he went to Africa he'd find a diamond the very first thing. A diamond as big as a

lump of sugar and he'd give it to his mom. No, he guessed he'd give it to Miss Hackett, his teacher. Miss Hackett was pretty and she was sure a lot better than old Crabpatch Wilson. Wow!

"Harbin Quadrangle!" his mother's voice sounded very impatient. "Your waffles are getting cold and soggy, the other children are all through breakfast and your daddy's ready to leave for the office. If you're not down here in two minutes I'm coming up."

Harbin sat up and reached down for the sock. He had it halfway on his foot when Mr. Pierce, the large black family dog, came into his room. "Well, hello, old boy," said Harbin letting go of his sock which now dangled from his toes. "Shake hands with me old boy."

Mr. Pierce wagged his tail and licked Harbin's face but he didn't want to shake hands. When Harbin reached for his paw he backed away. Harbin said, "Say, Mr. Pierce, I bet you've forgotten how to shake hands. Come on I'll teach you. Now first you sit. Sit boy! Come on, Mr. Pierce sit! MR. PIERCE SIT! Good boy. Now, give me your paw. No, don't lie down. Sit. Sit boy. Sit Mr. Pierce. SIT BOY! Come on, leggo my sock. Mr. Pierce, come back here with my sock. Mr. Pierce, come back here!"

But Mr. Pierce didn't. He trotted happily downstairs and laid Harbin's sock at Mr. Quadrangle's feet.

Mr. Quadrangle said, "What's this, Mr. Pierce, a blue grouse?" He picked up the sock and held it over Mr. Pierce's head. Mr. Pierce wagged his tail proudly.

Mrs. Quadrangle who was braiding Janey's hair said, "Let me see that sock a minute, Donald?"

Mr. Quadrangle handed it to her. She looked at it for a minute, told Janey to stand very still until she got back, then with the sock in her hand she marched out of the dining room and up the stairs.

In the meantime Harbin had fallen back on his bed and was lying in the jumbled mass of bedcovers and school clothes daydreaming about helping the Canadian Mounted Police capture the most dangerous criminal in all the world. Harbin also in uniform of course, because he was a secret member of the Mounties. Suddenly his mother's exasperated voice was saying, "Harbin Quadrangle, it's almost a quarter to eight and here you are not even half dressed. What's the matter with you?"

The brave little Mountie was jerked unceremoniously off the bed and clunked to the floor. "Now," said his mother. "Get dressed immediately, while I watch you."

Harbin fumbled around in the blankets for his tee shirt and sweater. Impatiently his mother pushed him out of the way and quickly found the clothes. Jerking the tee shirt then the sweater down over his head she said, "I certainly have enough to do in the morning without having to dress a great big eight-year-old boy. Now where are your jeans?"

"Well, uh, well uh," Harbin looked vaguely around his room.

His mother ripped the blankets off the bed and sure enough there were the jeans down by the foot. While Harbin put them on she went into the bathroom and filled the basin with warm water.

As soon as she was out of the room Harbin slumped back to the bed. "Wolves," he said to his shoe which he had picked up and was holding. "Boy wouldn't I love to have a wolf of my very own. I bet if I was nice to him and fed him meat and petted him a lot he'd be . . ." But he never found out what the wolf would be because his mother yanked him into the bathroom and began scrubbing his face and neck.

"Owwwwww, owwww, you're takin' the skin off," howled the brave little Mountie, trying to shield his face with both arms.

"Put your arms down," said his mother firmly. "You've still got some of Wednesday's chocolate ice cream up by your hairline. Now let me see your ears."

"Oh, gosh, not my ears! You scrub them so hard you make 'em ache."

"If they ache too much let me know and I'll give you an aspirin," said his mother briskly.

When she had him all scrubbed Mrs. Quadrangle rammed Harbin's feet into his socks and shoes and then scooted him down the stairs ahead of her.

When he came into the dining room his father said, "Well, if it isn't the fireman. One ring of the bell and he's in his clothes and down the pole."

Sylvia his sister who was eleven said, "Do all of our meals have to be ruined by that little slowpoke?"

Janey said, "I'm going to tell the kids at school that Mother has to dress you."

"You do and I'll . . ."

"You'll sit down and eat your waffles," said his mother. "Sylvia, run upstairs and get me an elastic band out of my desk. Janey, come here and I'll finish you—oh, quick, Donald, the baby's putting his dish on his head."

The baby, whom they called "Old-Timer," had indeed put his dish of oatmeal on his head. Little rivulets of milk and cereal ran down his forehead and into his eyes. He blinked and smiled happily. The children laughed uproariously. So did Mr. Quadrangle. Mrs. Quadrangle sighed and sent Harbin upstairs for a washrag. As he got slowly up from his chair, his mother shouted at him "Hurry! H-U-R-R-Y!" She spelled it out.

Harbin said, "I *am* hurrying," and shuffled from the room. He was all right, or rather he kept moving until he got to the stairs. In fact, to the first step, then suddenly the stairs turned into a rope ladder up the side of a ship. The ship was a pirate ship and Harbin who had swum under water clear across the ocean, was boarding her secretly, carefully, bravely. Hand over hand up the rope ladder.

When Mrs. Quadrangle finally sent Janey to see what in the world was the matter with Harbin, why he hadn't brought the washrag, Janey found him lying on the stairs pulling himself up by the balustrade, hand over hand, very slowly. When Janey saw him she yelled to her mother, "Mom, he hasn't even gone upstairs at all. He's just lying here in the hall."

Mrs. Quadrangle sighed and mopped Old-Timer off with the dishcloth. Mr. Quadrangle walked sternly out to the hall and said to Harbin who was halfway up the side of the pirate ship and so tired he didn't think he could go any farther, "What's going on out here? Why are you draped on the staircase like an old Spanish shawl?"

Then Harbin did a strange thing. He turned to his father and said, "Shhhh. They'll hear you."

Mr. Quadrangle looked at his son for a minute then went back into the dining room and said to his wife, "Call Dr. Watkins. The boy's hit his head and he's delirious."

"Oh, good heavens," said Mrs. Quadrangle dropping Old-Timer into his play pen with a thump. She ran into the front hall and sure enough there was Harbin clinging to the balustrade and breathing heavily. Mrs. Quadrangle rushed up and knelt beside him. "Son,

son are you all right?" she said laying her hand on his forehead.

"Of course I'm all right," said Harbin looking around at his assembled family. "What's the matter? Why are you all looking so funny?"

"Did you fall, son?" asked Mr. Quadrangle.

"Of course he did," said Mrs. Quadrangle impatiently. "But how far? Did you fall from the first or the third floor, sonny? And where do you hurt the most? Is it your back or your legs?"

"It's his back. He's broken it and he's completely paralyzed," announced Sylvia importantly. "I saw a movie once where a man broke his back and he acted just like Harbin."

"His arms look funny to me," said Janey. "See how funny the bones stick out?"

"There's nothin' wrong with my arms or my back," said Harbin sitting up. "I was just tryin' to go upstairs hand over hand the way sailors go up a rope."

His mother heaved a vast sigh of relief then said briskly, "All right everybody, into your coats, it's after 8:30. Janey get me Old-Timer's ski suit, it's in the hall closet."

Everybody was in the car, the engine was running and Mr. Quadrangle was saying impatiently, "If we don't leave right this instant I'll miss my train," when Janey suddenly remembered she had to bring two potatoes to school.

As Harbin was closest to the door Mrs. Quadrangle sent him to get the potatoes. "Now RUN FAST!" she told him. And he did—at least as far as the back porch where the potatoes were kept. Then he saw the old piece of fish net he had found on the beach the summer before. It was hanging on a nail right by the mop. Harbin stopped dead in his tracks. What was his fish net doin' here on the back porch? Ready for the garbage man?

Harbin jerked it off the nail intending to take it upstairs to his room. But somehow or another the feel of the net in his hands, the faint smell of seaweed that still clung to it made him think of the sea and oysters and pearls and pearl divers and giant clams. He had on his aqualung and was at the bottom of the ocean searching, searching for the famous pink pearl that would make him the richest man in all the world. It was dark and scary at the bottom of the ocean. And there were sharks and octopuses and baracuda and enormous snapping turtles and worst of all giant clams that could catch your leg in their giant shells and hold you there until you drowned, unless you were brave enough to cut off your own leg with your deep sea diving knife. "Ow, ow, the pain is awful!" Harbin said to himself as he looked down and saw his leg caught clear to the thigh in the shell of a giant clam. "I will have to cut off my leg but it is worth it because I have found the famous pink pearl and . . ."

"Harbin Quadrangle!" Sylvia yelled right in his ear. "You've probably made Daddy miss his train. What are you doing with that smelly old fish net and where are Janey's potatoes?"

"Uh, uh . . ." Harbin said looking in bewilderment at the fish net.

Pulling open the cooler door Sylvia grabbed two potatoes. "Come on," she said jerking Harbin by the arm. "Daddy's just furious."

Mr. Quadrangle missed his train all right and would have to take the 9:15. Also the first bell had already rung when the children got to school. Sylvia and Janey were panicky and hurled themselves out of the car and into the building. Not Harbin. He carefully collected his books, kissed his mother and Old-Timer, then ambled slowly across the schoolyard.

"Just look at that," said Mr. Quadrangle to Mrs. Quadrangle. "Not a care in the world. Plenty of time to look at the view. The second bell has probably rung but it means less than nothing to Hairbreadth Harbin the Human Rocket."

"You know, Don, I think maybe he needs thyroid pills," said Mrs. Quadrangle. "I *am* going to call Dr. Watkins. Just as soon as I get home."

"Go ahead," said Mr. Quadrangle. "But I'll bet he'll tell you there's nothing wrong with him that a little spanking won't cure. Anyway it's time for the train. Good-bye Old-Timer. Good-bye, honey, see you at 6:30."

As soon as she got home Mrs. Quadrangle called Dr. Watkins but he had gone to Oak Beach. Mrs. Quadrangle left word for him to call her when he got in and set to work to make an applesauce cake. Harbin loved applesauce cake and it was full of raisins and nuts and butter and sugar—all very nourishing and undoubtedly just the thing for a pitiful little boy with a very low thyroid.

As soon as she had the cake in the oven she called the butcher and ordered two soup bones with lots of marrow because she had heard that marrow was excellent for rundown people. She also made an enormous bowl of cherry jello—gelatine contains lots of protein—and whipped a full pint of cream. She was looking in her cookbook under the section "Feeding the Invalid" and wondering what else to fix for poor little Harbin, when Old-Timer announced via loud howls that it was time for his bath and morning nap.

After she had him bathed and settled in his crib with a bottle, she called Mr. Quadrangle at work and asked him to bring home a giant-sized bottle of cod-liver oil.

"What for?" asked Mr. Quadrangle. "Don't those vitamin pills we all take contain everything we need?"

"They're supposed to," said Mrs. Quadrangle, "but I don't want to take any chances with Harbin. He's so weak and rundown!"

"He's what?" asked Mr. Quadrangle.

"Weak and rundown," said Mrs. Quadrangle. "You certainly haven't forgotten how he lay on the stairs this morning, too feeble to go up or down."

Mr. Quadrangle sighed. "Any particular brand of cod-liver oil?" he said.

"Just get the strongest," said Mrs. Quadrangle. "The kind they use for invalids."

"How about a wheel chair, too?" said Mr. Quadrangle.

"Don't joke about it," said Mrs. Quadrangle. "It's serious."

"The way you're going on about this," Mr. Quadrangle said, "maybe I'd better exchange that wheel chair for a stretcher. By the way what did Dr. Watkins say?"

"He wasn't in," said Mrs. Quadrangle crossly. "He's going to call me."

"Fine," said Mr. Quadrangle. "Let me know what he says."

Then it was time for the children to come home from school. First Sylvia and her best friend Annabell came giggling in, fixed themselves two peanut butter and pickle sandwiches, two huge pieces of applesauce cake, and two enormous dishes of jello heaped with whipped cream. Loading their food on a tray they staggered up to Sylvia's room with it and spent the rest of the afternoon eating and giggling and telephoning.

Then Janey and her best friends, Mona and Kathy, came giggling in, grabbed some sandwiches and cake, Janey's, Harbin's, and Sylvia's rollerskates and left. There was no sign of Harbin.

She fed Old-Timer his applesauce and cookies, put on his ski suit and put him out in the yard in his pen. "You watch for your brother," she told him. "Let me know as soon as you see him coming and I'll walk down and help him."

Old-Timer intent on throwing all of his toys out of the pen as fast as he could, said, "Gogglewopshinogrit."

"All right," said his mother, "I trust you."

She went in the house and began fixing an enormous, really overpowering after-school snack for Harbin. Three thick peanut butter and pickle sandwiches, a chunk of cake big enough for Man Mountain Dean, and a soup bowl full of jello slogged over with whipped cream. When she had everything ready and laid out on the kitchen table she went to the window and looked anxiously down the street for Harbin.

He was there all right. Clear down by Mrs. Axle's and moving so slowly he looked almost like a statue. "Oh, the poor, poor little thing," said his mother grabbing her sweater off the kitchen chair and running out the back door. "Harbin, Harbin, wait for me," she called out, as she hurried down the street.

Harbin who was escaping from a dungeon and with terribly heavy leg chains on, was trying to feel his way along pitch black dank passageways that ran under the castle of the wicked bandit who had captured him, paid absolutely no attention to his mother.

Then he was being crushed in a rather hysterical embrace and his mother was saying, "Do you want Mother to carry you, sweetheart?"

"Carry me? You?" Harbin looked at his mother as if she had suddenly gone crazy.

"Of course, dear," she said crouching down and peering into his face. "Mother knows how tired and weak and sick you are."

"I'm not weak and sick," Harbin said irritably. "I feel fine."

"But you were moving so slowly," said his mother.

"Oh, I was just, well uh, . . . well, oh, lemme alone," Harbin finished in disgust.

But his mother put her arm around him and tried to lift him. Harbin struggled wildly and finally his mother dropped him. "Whatsa matter with you?" Harbin said angrily.

"Well if you won't let me carry you," said his mother, "I'll walk along with you in case you should feel faint. I made an applesauce cake today."

"Hot dog!" said Harbin. "That's my favorite."

"I know," said his mother with a catch in her voice.

"Can I have two pieces?" Harbin asked.

"Certainly," said his mother. "As many as you like."

"Oh, boy," said Harbin beginning to run.

"Harbin, Harbin, darling," called his mother anxiously. "Be careful. You'll wear yourself out."

She needn't have worried. Harbin ran as far as the Wilcox's hedge then suddenly he saw the Wilcox's yellow cat, Dandelion, hiding behind the hedge. Harbin stopped short. "A lion. A full-grown vicious lion with a bullet in its shoulder and a little native child between its paws." The natives in the village had sent Harbin, armed only with a bow and arrow, out to save the chief's little son. Slowly carefully he crouched down. Then just as slowly and carefully he took an arrow out of his quiver, put it in his bow and began to pull back the string. He was just getting ready to let it snap when an arm grabbed him around the waist and his mother's voice said, "Son, son, what is the matter? Have you got a cramp in your stomach?"

"Oh, Mom," said Harbin disgustedly. "Why can't you lemme alone?"

"But your face was contorted with pain," his mother said.

"It was not," Harbin said. "I was just, well I was just, I mean I was practisin' shootin' a bow and arrow."

"Well, come along and get your cake," said his mother. "I have everything laid out on the kitchen table."

"Keen," said Harbin actually hurrying the rest of the way home.

When they got to the house Old-Timer who had thrown all his toys out and had nothing to play with held out his arms and whimpered to be picked up. Mrs. Quadrangle decided to take him out and let him run around while Harbin ate his little lunch. She put the baby on the grass and sat on the steps to watch him.

When Harbin walked into the kitchen and saw the enormous feast his mother had laid out for him he said, "At last, at last," and fell into the chair and began shoveling in the food because all afternoon he had been on a desert island without anything to eat but a few raw fish he caught with his hands and then just by chance when he was so weak he could hardly drag himself along the beach, he sighted this boat and they took him aboard and the cook fixed all this wonderful food and as he had eaten and gotten back his strength he was going to tell them about the uranium mine he had found. Harbin closed his eyes. The room began to go round and round. He felt terrible. Like a steer that had been roped around the stomach. He loosened his belt. That made him feel a little better but the kitchen seemed awfully hot. Slowly wearily he got up and went outdoors.

His mother still sitting on the steps, looked at him and said, "Harbin, honey, you look awful. Are you sick?"

"Well, I guess I am," Harbin said, slumping down beside her.

"Stick out your tongue," his mother demanded.

He did. She said, "Just as I thought. Your tongue is coated and your throat is red. You go right upstairs and get into bed. I'm going to ask Dr. Watkins to drop by."

Taking his belt off altogether made Harbin feel much better—so did his cool bed. He went to sleep. It was after supper when he woke up. He could tell because the house smelled faintly of lamb stew, he could hear Janey and Sylvia and the neigborhood kids quarreling over whose turn it was to be *it* in hide-and-go-seek. He turned over and closed his eyes again. There were steps on the stairs and Dr. Watkins boomed out, "Hi, there, sonny, what's the trouble?"

"Nothing," said Harbin. "I guess I just ate too much."

After Dr. Watkins had peered in his ears, nose and throat, poked and thumped him all over and pronounced him "sound as a nut," Mrs. Quadrangle who had been hovering anxiously in the background, said, "Dr. Watkins I want to talk to you." She took him downstairs and told him in full detail about Harbin's spells of weakness.

He said, "Nothing physically wrong with the boy. Let's see, he's going on nine isn't he?"

"Yes, he'll be nine next September," Mrs. Quadrangle said sadly as though Harbin would never live to see his birthday cake.

"Well, then," said Dr. Watkins fishing in his pocket for a prescription blank, "I would diagnose his trouble as extra acute daydreaming. Now, I'll write out this prescription and I'm pretty sure if you follow it, he'll be back to normal in no time." He wrote rapidly on a prescription blank, folded it and handed it to Mrs. Quadrangle. Then he was gone.

Taking the slip of paper Mrs. Quadrangle went into Mr. Quadrangle's study and said, "It's just as I thought, Donald. Harbin is sick. Dr. Watkins gave me a prescription for him."

"Let's see it," said Mr. Quadrangle.

Mrs. Quadrangle handed it to him. He unfolded it and read, "Call Mrs. Piggle-Wiggle. Vinemaple 1-2345."

"Mrs. Piggle-Wiggle!" exclaimed Mrs. Quadrangle.

"Certainly," said Mr. Quadrangle. "She's earned a pretty fine reputation for curing children of irritating faults. Let's give it a try."

"Well, you call her then," said Mrs. Quadrangle. "I wouldn't know what to say."

"Very well," said Mr. Quadrangle picking up the phone and dialing the number. "Hello, Mrs. Piggle-Wiggle, this is Harbin Quadrangle's father. I just wondered if you knew of anything that would help cure a slowpoke?"

Apparently Mrs. Piggle-Wiggle did know because

there was a silence on Mr. Quadrangle's end of the phone for quite a while, then he said, "Thank you very much, I'll be right over."

"What did she say? Where are you going? Can she cure Harbin?" asked Mrs. Quadrangle.

Mr. Quadrangle stood up, gave her a kiss and said, "It's in the bag." He was whistling as he went out the front door.

When he came back about half an hour later he was carrying a small bottle of clear fluid and a little sprayer.

"What is that?" asked Mrs. Quadrangle who was in the living room reading a book on child psychology.

"Mrs. Piggle-Wiggle said to spray his clothes with it. She said to lay out the clothes he will wear to school tomorrow and then spray them thoroughly, especially the shoes."

"But what will the spray do, what is it for?" asked Mrs. Quadrangle anxiously.

"Dunno," said Mr. Quadrangle humming "Yankee Doodle." "But let's get started." He uncorked the bottle and filled the little sprayer.

When they went into his room they found Harbin deeply asleep. His mother quickly felt his forehead but it was cool and moist. He appeared very relaxed and he was smiling. Apparently his dream was a happy one.

Tiptoeing over to the bureau Mrs. Quadrangle opened drawers and took out clean underclothes, socks, jeans, tee shirt and a sweater. She laid them out on the foot of Harbin's bed and Mr. Quadrangle sprayed them thoroughly. They were tiptoeing out when Mr. Quadrangle remembered the shoes and went back and sprayed them.

Mrs. Quadrangle didn't sleep very well that night. The minute she got out of bed the next morning she rushed into Harbin's room to see if he was all right. He was still fast asleep. She tiptoed out, went downstairs and put on the coffee.

Mr. Pierce scratched on the cellar door. She opened it and he wagged his tail and she patted him on the head and then she put him out. It was raining. A thin misty cold drizzle. Mr. Pierce looked at her reproachfully and tried to squeeze past her back into the house.

She said firmly, "Oh, no you don't, sir. You've been in the house all night and now I want you to take a little run." She tried to push him with her foot but he sat down heavily on it. She had just about decided to give up when suddenly the back door was flung open and Harbin fully dressed, and combed and washed, said briskly, "Whatsa matter, Mom? What are you tryin' to do?"

"It's Mr. Pierce," said Mrs. Quadrangle giving him another yank. "He won't go out and take his morning run, because it's raining and he hates the rain."

"Whatsa matter old boy," said Harbin kneeling beside him, "don't you like the rain?"

Mr. Pierce thumped his tail on the porch and licked Harbin's face.

Standing up Harbin said, "I'll go with him, Mom. We'll take a run around the block."

"But the rain," said Mrs. Quadrangle. "You'll get all wet."

"Not me," said Harbin. "I'll run too fast. You just watch."

He jumped off the porch skipping the steps entirely and raced down the driveway. Yelping happily Mr. Pierce followed. Mrs. Quadrangle went into the kitchen, put the milk on for the cocoa and poured herself a cup of coffee.

She had only taken two sips when the back door flew open and in came Harbin and Mr. Pierce. Harbin's cheeks were bright pink, his eyes sparkled and neither he nor Mr. Pierce seemed to be at all wet.

"My goodness," his mother said, "you must have run faster than the wind."

"Faster than the rain, you mean," said Harbin laughing. "Boy, I've never run so fast. Even Mr. Pierce couldn't keep up with me. What are we having for breakfast, I'm starved."

Mrs. Quadrangle, who didn't really wake up all the way until after she had had her coffee, said, "Well, uh, uh . . ."

"I know," said Harbin briskly. "We'll have French toast."

"Good idea," said his mother. "I'll get at it just as soon as I finish this cup of coffee."

"I'll make it," said Harbin. "You just tell me what to do." He flung open a cupboard and began rattling the pots and pans.

"Get out a bowl," said his mother, "and the eggs and some milk and . . ."

There was a sharp rapping at the back door.

It was Georgie Wilcox, the paper boy. He said he was sorry he was so late—but he had a flat tire on his bicycle, and here was the paper he hoped it hadn't gotten too wet while he was fixing his bike.

Harbin put down the mixing bowl he had taken out of the pan cupboard and said, "Hey, Georgie, want me to come along and help you deliver? I can take one side of the street and you take the other."

Georgie, who remembered Harbin as something of a human snail, said quickly, "Oh, that's all right, Harbin, I'll make it I guess."

Harbin said, "You can't. It's almost six-thirty."

Mrs. Quadrangle looked up at the kitchen clock, then wiped her eyes on her apron and looked again. It *was* only 6:25—heavens she and Harbin must have gotten up about 5:45. She looked at Harbin in astonishment. Could this bright-eyed eager little boy be the same one who always was the last to breakfast—in fact the last for everything?

Harbin said, "Wait a sec till I get my jacket, Georgie."

Georgie who looked sleepy and as messy as if he had dressed in a wind tunnel said, "Well, okay, but hurry."

In two seconds Harbin was back with the jacket. As he went out the door he said to his mother, "Better make a huge batch of French toast, Mom. Come on, Mr. Pierce. We got work to do."

When Mr. Quadrangle came downstairs a little after seven-thirty his first words were "What about the magic spray? Did it work?"

"I got up so early and have been so busy I forgot all about it," said Mrs. Quadrangle. "Now sit down and eat this French toast while it's hot. Did you waken the girls?"

"I think they're both up," said Mr. Quadrangle. "But what about Harbin? Have you called him yet?"

"Called him?" said Mrs. Quadrangle. "He was downstairs before six o'clock."

"Where is he now?" asked Mr. Quadrangle. "Dawdling some place I'll bet."

"He is not," said Mrs. Quadrangle. "Look out, that plate's hot as the dickens."

"Well then where is he?" asked his father impatiently.

"He's gone with Georgie Wilcox on his paper route. Georgie had a flat tire on his bicycle and was late and Harbin offered to help him."

"Hope Georgie's customers won't mind a morning paper being delivered in the afternoon," said Mr. Quadrangle through a bite of French toast.

Just then the back door burst open and Harbin called out, "Sure hope breakfast is ready. I'm starvinger than a lion." Seeing his father he said, "Hi, Dad. Say, know what? Georgie Wilcox said I'm the fastest helper he's ever had on his paper route and he said if his mom and dad let him go to California to visit his grandmother this summer he'll let me take over his paper route and he makes almost *forty dollars a month*. Zowie."

"But you'd have to get up so *early*," said his mother.

"Who cares?" said Harbin. "I'd make almost *forty dollars a month!*"

"You make forty dollars a month?" sneered Sylvia who had just come to the table. "Don't be fantastic. A slowpoke like you wouldn't be worth forty cents."

"Sylvia," said Mr. Quadrangle sternly, "be quiet. Now, son, what about this paper route? Do you think you could handle it?"

"Of course I could," Harbin said. "Gosh, this morning I delivered three papers to Georgie's one."

Mrs. Quadrangle said, "Where's Janey? Was she up when you came downstairs, Sylvia?"

"I don't know," said Sylvia. "I called her about thirty thousand times but when I went into her room to get my blue sweater she sneaked and wore and spilled Coke all down the front of, she was still in bed reading."

"I'd better call again," said Mrs. Quadrangle. She went to the foot of the stairs and called "Janey. Jaaaaaeeeeeee!"

After a while a muffled voice answered, "Be down in a sec."

Mrs. Quadrangle listened for a minute, then hearing no signs of activity from Janey's room she went up. She found Janey still in her nightgown leaning on the window sill and looking out at the rain. Her mother said quite sharply, "Janey Quadrangle, it is almost time to leave for school. Why aren't you dressed?"

Janey turned, gave her mother a dreamy faraway look and said, "Rain running down the window pane reminds me of tears. Do you think that rain could be the tear drops of all the poor people who have died?"

"My goodness what a morbid idea," said Mrs. Quadrangle pulling Janey's skirt and sweater out of the jumble of bedclothes. "Here put these on quickly then I'll start on your hair while you put on your shoes and socks."

Slowly Janey straightened up, took the skirt and sweater from her mother and then said, "Mother, if I should die would you and Daddy cry?"

"Don't talk that way," said her mother crossly. "In fact don't talk at all. Just hurry."

"But Mother," said Janey, "what if I did die tomorrow? What if I got run over by a truck?"

With an exasperated sigh Mrs. Quadrangle grabbed the skirt and sweater from Janey. "Come here," she said. "I'll dress you. Although I think it is perfectly ridiculous for a great big girl to have to be dressed by her mother." She had just begun to pull the skirt down over Jancy's hcad whcn suddenly she remembered the little blower filled with Mrs. Piggle-Wiggle's magic liquid for slowpokes. She pulled the skirt off Janey's head, picked up her sweater, shoes and socks and said, "You go start getting washed, I'll be right back."

The little blower was in the drawer of Mr. Quadrangle's bedside stand. She took it out and carefully sprayed Janey's clothes. Then she went back to Janey's room where Janey instead of washing her face was lying across the bed singing "My country 'tis of thee." When she saw her mother she said, "I know all the verses to 'The Star Spangled Banner,' want to hear them?"

"No!" said her mother firmly. "Stand up so I can dress you."

She jammed the skirt and sweater down over Janey's

head. Stuffed her feet into her socks and shoes, then pushed her into the bathroom, washed her face and hands and was just braiding her hair when Mr. Quadrangle called, "Molly, I'll have to leave for the station in five minutes."

"All right, dear," said Mrs. Quadrangle snapping an elastic around the end of one of Janey's braids. To Janey she said, "You'll just have to eat some toast and peanut butter on the way to the station, now scoot and fix it while I get Old-Timer up."

"But he hasn't had his mush," said Janey who suddenly seemed very wide awake and bright.

"I know," said Mrs. Quadrangle, "but we're late so he'll just have to wait."

"I'll fix him some mush in a bottle," said Janey. "You change him and put on his ski suit and I'll fix the bottle and we'll give it to him in the car."

When they were all settled in the car complete with Sylvia's note for an early dismissal to go to the dentist, with Uncle Joe's elephant tooth for Harbin to show during natural history period, Janey with Old-Timer and the bottle, Mr. Quadrangle said, "Okay everybody?"

"Okay," they all said.

"All aboard then," he shouted stepping on the gas. "Next stop the station."

Then he turned to Mrs. Quadrangle and said, "Say did you by any chance spray any of that magic stuff on my clothes, I feel awfully quick and alert for this early in the morning."

Smiling a little sheepishly Mrs. Quadrangle said, "Only a little bit on your shoes."

"Then we're even," laughed Mr. Quadrangle. "I sprayed some on your hair when you were asleep."

"No wonder I woke up so early," laughed Mrs. Quadrangle.

"Let's all sing 'God Bless America,'" said Harbin, from the back seat.

"Let's all sing 'God Bless Mrs. Piggle-Wiggle,'" said Mr. Quadrangle, honking the horn at a fat gray pigeon.